1

Dirty Work
A review of Ian Rankin's John Rebus books

Dirty Work

A review of Ian Rankin's John Rebus books

Ray Dexter & Nadine Carr

A Spinderella Paperback

First published in Great Britain in 2015

By Spinderella

2 3 4 5 6 7 8 9 10 11 12

Copyright © Ray Dexter 2015

The right of Ray Dexter and Nadine Carr to be identified as the authors of this work has been asserted by them in accordance with the Copyright, Designs and Patents Act 1988.

A CIP catalogue record for this book is available from the British Library

ISBN: 978-1-326-41521-1

For Aron and Maja, as always

"That's what I've been trying to do. It's this sort of very long-term project. I mentioned James Joyce before. He once said of *Ulysses* that he tried to recreate Dublin so that if the city ever disappeared, they could build it again brick by brick just by reading his novel. I feel like that about the Rebus series. If Edinburgh were to disappear in a puff of smoke, you could bring it back to life using my books as a template."

Ian Rankin 2002

Introduction

Relax, this'll be short. You know how it works, you buy a book like this and there's a huge introduction that you skip past because you want to get to the proper part of the book. When you've read this book, and if you've enjoyed it then go back and read the afterword which will serve as an introduction. If you are a minority reader, who likes introductions you can find your way to the back: the rest of you just turn the page.

Oh, one final thing, the books are in chronological publication order...

Enjoy.

Knots & Crosses

Published by: The Bodley Head (1987)

One line summary: We get to meet John Rebus for the first time, and he's on the trail of a weirdly-motivated serial killer.

Cover: The original cover was a sort of noughts and crosses, with matches for the crosses and knots for the noughts. Later reprints went for the rather irrelevant Celtic cross gravestone (which we concede has a sort of know and cross motif), or some typical Edinburgh steps, or minimalist used matchstick heads.

TV adaptation: The last episode of the Ken Stott's last season was entitled Knots and Crosses but had absolutely nothing to do with this story, apart from the name, and some of the knot and cross-based clues.

Four things to notice about Knots and Crosses:

1) Not surprisingly even Ian Rankin says this is his least favourite Rebus book. In *The Guardian* in 2012 he wrote: "it reads like it was written when I was a postgraduate literature student. I wasn't inside Rebus's head; he was just a cipher to get me through the story." We'll go into the details of this a lot more in the Background section below...

2) This is a fictional Edinburgh. Rankin wasn't really writing about Edinburgh at this early stage, he was just **not** writing about his home town, where his first book was set (the non-Rebus starring *The Flood*). So the police station and many of the other locations are fiction. It was only later that Rankin realised that a) realism was cool b) realism was a lot easier to write than creating something from scratch.

3) The character of Rebus has a number of sources. Most will be detailed in the Background but Rankin has written and spoken about this a lot. As his intention wasn't to create a detective series the exact sequence of events is unclear and has become a story to wheel out at interviews and conventions. We'll try to get to the bottom of it in the Background section.

4) Most significant perhaps is that in this book is the only time we get even the vaguest description of John Rebus. He is described as having slightly less brown and slightly less green eyes than his brother. Uncoincidently (sic) this is the same as Rankin. Rankin won't describe Rebus again, so Rebus looks how you want him to. If you're desperate you won't go far wrong by getting the most recent photograph of Ian Rankin you can find and imagine he had let himself go...

Firsts and Lasts:

Obviously this is the first time we meet 40 year-old John Rebus, his stage-hypnotist brother Michael, his ex-wife Rhona (though Rebus doesn't actually encounter her himself) and his daughter Sam. We also meet other characters who will be back in various forms: DI Gill Templer, who will be a major figure, their relationship always tainted by the events here. We also meet Jim Stevens, who also turns up in *Watchman*, Rankin's next book, which isn't about Rebus, but also in later novels. Also DS Jack Morton is here, a bit part player but worth noting.

This is the only time we see Rebus (pre-retirement) as anything but a Detective Inspector. Here he is a lowly DS, doing spade work and routine desk duties. He gets a promotion after the events of this book, although the timing is a bit weird, as we'll see. We get our first description of Rebus's apartment on Arden St, Marchmont, although it isn't named as such yet. And unsurprisingly, given this was supposed to be a stand-alone book, this is the only time we get to really delve into Rebus's past, with a lot of his SAS history retold. This is also the first time Rebus drinks in the Sutherland, a real pub, although he doesn't appear to be a regular.

This is the first of the 'something and something' titles; it is also the first one with a loose connection to a game. And this is the first of many, many times where Rankin's life and family history merges into Rebus's. Rebus's father died on Rankin's birthday, 28th April.

Background:

Rankin describes the time he wrote this clearly in the re-print published in the early noughties. He was a twenty-four year old postgraduate English Literature student, with a grant and plenty of time to write. It was March 1985 and he had just signed his first book contract (for *The Flood*) with a minor publisher. A few things were nagging at him. He'd set *The Flood* in Cardenden (pronounced Carden**den**, like you say the words garden and den as one word – gardenden), Fife, where Rankin (and Rebus) both originate from, and people he knew from his home village were asking whether they were in it. He wanted to avoid that with his next book. In addition, although Rankin had designs on being a 'proper' literary author he was having second thoughts. He had given his father a James Kelman book (whom he was studying). His father said he didn't think it was even written in English. It made Rankin rethink what sort of writer he wanted to be. Rankin claims the idea for *Knots and Crosses* came to him on the day of the contract signing, "In (my) head from page 1 to circa page 250." He also claims with hindsight that Rebus came to him as a fully formed character, "with fragile sanity". He made him older because of plot reasons, and to distance himself from his age group and the cliché of 'writing what you know'. He made a note in the margin 'The hero maybe a cop.'

12

Rankin wrote the book that summer when he should have been reading Muriel Spark. He has spent most of the last thirty years rather romantically claiming he wrote it in his bedsit at 24 Arden St, Marchmont, staring out of the window across the street. He decided Rebus should live in the apartment he could see over the road (we've always liked to think that Rebus's constant acknowledgement of students in neighbouring flats in later books is a nod to the young Mr. Rankin). The truth is that although Rankin did live at number 24 by the time he wrote the book in the summer of 1986 he had moved to the New Town and was housemates with another student called John Curt (ring a bell?) who worked at the Oxford bar (double ring a bell?).

Rankin was rather lucky; there was no competition, no alternatives, no precedents with Edinburgh detectives but as he wrote he realised (in his own words) that he was "too young and too stupid" to write this type of book. He knew nothing about police procedure and even less about the rules of crime fiction. He solved the first problem by writing to the Lothian and Borders Chief Constable to ask for help and being directed to a couple of CID detectives at the police station in Leith. As Rankin tells it, his questions led him to be suspect number 350 in a real child abduction case.

"What I didn't know at the time was that this police station was investigating a child abduction, which was very similar to what I was describing; eventually, seven kids were taken and killed. These cops see a lunatic come into the station with this spurious story about writing a novel and they immediately cast me as a suspect. But they're very clever. They said to me, "Well, you want to see how an investigation works?" And I said, "Yeah, I'd love that." So they start asking me all these questions, and typing in my answers, and I think I'm getting a great story, lots of local colour. Then, eventually, they get to the question, "What were you doing on the night of the 11th of November?" I'm playing along with them, and I say, "I don't know, I think I was drunk that night." And that gets typed in, too. Well, it wasn't till I went home that weekend and told my dad the story, that he said, "You silly bugger, they think you've done it." And I went back and asked the police, and sure enough, I was a suspect - they were looking at me as a kidnapper."

Now this anecdote is a little coloured by storytelling licence, which is a hallmark of Rankin's interviews but police *were* looking into the disappearance and murder in 1983 of little Caroline Hogg, who was one of many victims of vile serial killer Robert Black, originally from Scotland. Back to Rankin:

"(The real culprit) was eventually caught, down in England. And this is one of those coincidences that you couldn't put into a novel, because nobody would believe you. It seems some guy was cutting his grass with an old lawnmower and a stone caught in the blade, so he bent down to fix it. As he bent down, he happened to look to the edge of the lawn, where he had a hedge. And beneath the hedge he saw a child's feet and a man's feet, and he saw the child's feet suddenly lift up -- and heard a little squeal. Later, the man went inside, and he saw this van driving away. So he took down the number and phoned the police. The police found the van, pulled it over, and in the back of the van, there was a rolled-up carpet - and the carpet was moving. That was victim number eight, right there." Again, there are some slight re-telling problems here with the truth. For example when Black was caught, the girl was actually bundled into a sleeping bag.

As Rankin wrote he was aware of another problem that was harder to solve. He didn't see himself as a crime author, and wasn't a huge fan. He felt William McIlvanney, a credible Scottish author would be an influence because he had written gritty thrillers in the 1970s. So he set out to write a thriller in that sort of style, claiming to not even know book shops had special crime sections, although for such a bookworm we'll take that with a large pinch of salt. What is certain is that Rankin never really did become a classic crime writer. In his words again, "I write commentaries on Scotland's present, its foibles, and psychoses, the flaws in its character. I'm

14

dissecting a nation", which is bang on. At the time of this though he DEFINITELY wasn't a crime writer and he wasn't really commentating on Scotland either, save for a lovely author-voiced comment about tramps in the library.

Rankin has also implied that the name John Rebus is a bit of a millstone. He now thinks it's a stupid name, but at the time he thought he was being clever! A rebus is a kind of pictorial puzzle that uses pictures to make phrases. If you've ever seen the gameshow *Catchphrase* then you've seen a Rebus. They're also called Dingbats, but John Dingbat really is a silly name. So Rebus's name was literally a puzzle. He also claims the "John" came from the Ernest Tidyman's John Shaft detective books, which he loved (yet he claims to not read crime novels!). Later Rankin would make Rebus a third generation Polish immigrant, which just about works.

Rankin had ambitions to be a professor of English, and admired the clever books of Umberto Eco. The postgrad literary student, who loved Eco's literary criticism, coming from the left-field to crime fiction thought he'd make the whole thing a puzzle - ha ha. He liked the idea of the wordplay and the book as a puzzle.

Looking back now Rankin isn't a fan of his writing, cringing at his nods to all the writers he admired at the time. He couldn't believe his books were put in the crime section either – he thought they were literary works.

As far as the plot goes Rankin claims he wanted to write a contemporary version of Robert Louis Stevenson's *The Case of Dr Jekyll and Mr. Hyde,* especially as he felt that novella should really have been set in Edinburgh, not London. He also hints at the real-life story of Deacon Brodie, whom Stevenson was also fascinated by. The plot, as written has very little to do with either, save for the mild-mannered, well-respected gentleman by day, sociopath by night (almost) clichéd character. Although, as a throw-away line in some interviews Rankin implies that Rebus himself was the Jekyll/Hyde persona, and this theme does seep through, even in the final draft. You can see how Jekyll and Hyde seeded this, but it's hard to really spot in the book we see.

The more obvious source is that this was an era where the serial-killer was becoming a big feature in contemporary storytelling. Although not a serial killer per se, *Nightmare on Elm Street* had been a big hit the year before, with a dream-generated child stalker and killer. Surely postgrad students went to the movies? Also, more tenuously, would bookish Rankin have read the first work of the other great Scottish writer of his generation? Iain Banks' *The Wasp Factory* had been out only a few months. It's a ghastly, gruesome tale of a child serial killer (mainly of animals) but would Rankin have wanted to see what his opposition was up to? You bet! We shall stop speculating, but with the very real Robert Black also on the prowl this was topical stuff.

Rankin felt the Jekyll link wasn't spotted by reviewers and readers at the time so he'll try this all again with the next book, and really lay it on with a jam spreader...

Oh, and finally this was meant to be a stand-alone novel with themes, not the first book of a series about a Scottish policeman, and Rankin killed Rebus off in the first draft, and even the version we have here the ending is ambiguous to say the least.

Things That Don't Make Sense:

Quite a lot of it if we're being blunt. It's not being disloyal to say this Rebus is unrecognizable to the character known to millions. He's very religious, reading passages of the Bible for comfort (!), he has a tape deck (!) and plays jazz (!!) (although many crime writers get their hero's music wrong at first, see Mark Billingham, and Peter Robinson). He is a voracious reader and can quote *King Lear* from memory. He also has a huge knowledge of Dostoyevsky and can tell the whole story of *Crime and Punishment*: essentially Rankin was writing himself again. He has yet to let Rebus free to write his own character. In fact Rankin often says he's too scared to talk about Rebus for fear he'll disappear in a puff of smoke.

And despite this being a stand-alone novel with Rebus as a possible suspect all the way along the writing never allows us to really suspect him, despite the weird locked room in his apartment.

The whole hypnosis plot strand is horribly contrived and this family business is almost never mentioned again.

How did Rebus know the result of a boxing match that a colleague was going to watch in the pub in the evening? When did it actually take place? Most boxing matches take place late at night, so was it the night before? We know it was the 1980s and some sport wasn't shown live (see the classic *Whatever Happened to the Likely Lads* about precisely that) but even if that was the case surely nobody would be stupid enough to bet on a match that had already happened?

In addition, although we're trying to be nice the entire plot itself makes little sense. From the lack of witnesses to the abductions, let alone the clues Rebus does not follow up on, and direct communications from the killer to him via the knots and crosses in the title. We know why; Rankin wants us to doubt Rebus, but *our* Rebus wouldn't do that. And anyway why would the killer go to all the trouble he goes to get Rebus's attention? And he was rather lucky the victims had the names they had...

This is a little harsh but the party scene where Rebus meets Gill Templer is a little studenty in nature, and not the sort of party real grown-ups go to. We'll blame Rankin's age and lack of worldly experience…

Why was Rebus, a detective sergeant in CID doing a night shift of paper work?

And finally the SAS is not the Special Air Squadron, it's Special Air Service! And how did DCI Anderson know about the tunnels below the library?

Music References:

Well there aren't any, apart from some late night jazz, probably by Stan Getz on a cassette!

Review

Knots & Crosses is a tale that contains a character called John Rebus but this isn't our John Rebus and this almost shouldn't be part of the series. It's like the original *Star Trek* pilot, things aren't quite right. Rankin is obviously forgiven for not knowing how life was going to pan out, but other writers have got it spot on first time. Look at the first Jack Reacher book. Lee Child delivers almost the best one in the series first time, save for Reacher's weird blues obsession…

But it's not just the music taste, Rebus is just…wrong. You can actually count the Rebusy moments on one hand: when he spoils his colleague's evening in the pub by revealing the winner of a boxing match, and the brilliant scene where Rebus pulls apart the arguments of the posh girl collecting money for the Workers' Revolutionary Party. Aside from that we have a Rebus who is devout, goes on fly-fishing trips, and would rather walk home after a shift than drive his car. He drinks coffee at home, listens to jazz on a tape deck. This is a horny Rebus, a Rebus that blacks out from over-work, I mean, please.

So, although the plot is perfectly reasonable for a forgettable 1980's pulp fiction stand-alone novel, it tries to do too many things and fails to do any of them well. It's a serial killer story which lacks the gory details to make the horror fans enjoy it; Rankin is not part of the horror scene and is too squeamish to do what Stephen King says is the essence of horror: create characters you love then do horrible things to them. As a police procedural tale it's woeful. Rebus doesn't do any sleuthing until page 95 and even that happens off-stage, as Rebus finds a link to a pale blue car (apparently), so crime fans will be left wanting. Even if Rankin was

18

going for his suggested literary puzzle concept well it doesn't do that very well either, with not enough cleverness to pull the reader out of the tale to see the joke. He even uses the word 'manumission' for heaven's sake! We've discussed Rebus's name, but the knots and crosses clues given to Rebus, as well as the name and the pseudonym of the baddie (go look it up, but it comes across not really clever but more, 'oh for heavens' sake'). This is, in essence a story about revenge that happens to feature a policeman, but could have equally starred a postman or a truck driver. And it's pretty obvious who the final victim is planned to be. The ending is horribly rushed too; ultimately Rebus's fate is left in the balance because he was never meant to be a recurring character. In fact, Jim Stevens, who does appear in Rankin's next book, gets the final chapter, unlikeable though he is. The hypnosis angle is also forced into the story to drive it and explain the entire story. And the SAS backstory will jar with the Rebus we know and love all the way through the series. Rankin rightly and conveniently lets a lot of this disappear, to be forgotten, and in some ways, so should this book. This is a curiosity, nothing more.

Luckily for us, Rankin, the genius is learning his craft and there are flashes. Read the library scene, which is unfortunately in what is known as the omniscient point of view (POV) and you can see the true voice of this wonderful series beginning to emerge. He just wasn't quite ready yet. Many claim to like this, but as Rankin has noted, it barely caused a ripple on release, except for one review in the Glasgow Herald, which Rankin noted, barely had a word of praise: 'Bastard, Bastard, Bastard!' he wrote. Michael Menzel (a random reviewer on amazon.com) called it the worst book he'd ever read, which is a bit harsh. Do approach with caution though; if it's your first one, then keep reading, please. If you come to it late, expect a weird ride.

Hide and Seek

Published by: Barrie and Jenkins (1991)

One Line summary: Rebus returns, behaving like Rebus, investigating the suspicious death of a heroin addict in a squalid squat; the case leads to bigger, more powerful people and their strange ideas of entertainment.

Cover: Pentangles, the good old 'chiller' font, the Edinburgh skyline under a blood-red sky. Subsequent editions seem to focus on park railings.

TV Adaptation: None

Four things to notice about Hide and Seek:

1) Rebus is back and has a complete personality change, we'll come back to this in the Background section but this is so different as to be remarkable on its own, but the four-year gap between books helps explain this partly. It's so different that you could actually read *Hide and Seek* at any time and not know it was number two. *Knots and Crosses* could never be classified like that.

2) Rankin felt this was a real companion piece to *Knots and Crosses*; he wanted people to really get the whole Jekyll and Hyde thing and felt people hadn't noticed it in *Knots*. This time Rankin wasn't going to allow the reader to miss the references. Each chapter starts with a quote from the novella (OK, OK he doesn't reference the quotes); Rebus fails to read the book in the evenings; a suicide note directly quotes from the book, although again it isn't referenced. Also the character names are lifted from the text: Enfield (where *Jekyll* starts, and just up the road from where Rankin was living), Poole, Carew, Lanyon, and

20

Vanderhyde for heaven's sake! In truth, one gets the feeling Rankin hadn't got rid of his desire for Umberto Eco-like playfulness, with Brian Holmes' surname, Superintendent Watson and every possible permutation on the synonym "Hyde/Hide."

3) Edinburgh is still a fictional city but we're starting to see the way the future's is going to go. We're imagining Rankin's thought processes here but he'd written one Rebus book and now it was time to do it again. He now knew he was writing about an Edinburgh cop, but what would give him an edge. His conclusion was realism, not cozy Edinburgh realism but horrible, crime-ridden Edinburgh and this is why we see a lot of the Pilmuir Estate. In later interviews Rankin would firm up his philosophy and note that Oxfam's first UK work was in Edinburgh and that was the Edinburgh he wanted to write about. This dark side would always be a part of the series and would culminate with that glorious line in *The Falls*, which we won't spoil by mentioning here.

Firsts and Lasts:

This marks the first appearance of Detective Superintendent Thomas 'Farmer' **Watson**, although based on what he's doing perhaps his rank should be a little higher; this will be changed in later books as Rankin starts to take these things more seriously. Watson's first appearance also brings the first of the now legendary police nicknames, although this isn't one of the best. We also meet DC Brian **Holmes**, working as a reluctant sidekick for Rebus, Holmes' girlfriend Nell Stapleton, who'll be back as well. This is the only time Holmes is a DC, promoted next time we see him. It's also the first of two appearances by blind man Nicholas Vanderhyde. "Mrs. Cochrane downstairs" gets her first mention too. This is also the first time we meet Rebus as a Detective Inspector, a rank he will keep until retirement.

The cynical will say this is the first real time we get a lot of big coincidences holding the plot together. It's the last time Rebus seems to solely appreciate jazz, listens to the classical music station Radio 3 and enjoys wine as a tipple of choice. It's also the last time Rankin gives us 'meaningful' character names. It's a first and rare occasion for Rebus acknowledging a previous case, with a couple of vague mentions of the case in *Knots and Crosses*. It's the first time we get the classic Rankin day-to-day chapter headings

Oh, and it's the first time Rebus gets suspended, but at least this time it's a little unfair. Finally, it's the first time Rankin uses the word trellis table incorrectly, when he means to use trestle table.

Background:

Knots and Crosses had been published to little acclaim, and Rankin tried his hand at two different types of book in the interim. One was published as *The Watchman*, a Le Carre-like thriller. Again, it wasn't a big hit. He also wrote *Westwind*, a techno-thriller set in the USA. It was published at the time but it's the one Rankin book that he refuses to reissue, so it'll cost you if you want a copy. Rankin claims in his diary on June 14th 1986 that he wanted to write either Rebus 2 or *The Watchman. The Watchman* won, but this might have been because there was vague interest in making a television drama out of *Knots and Crosses*. The delay while this never happened pushed *Watchman* to the fore.

Watchman was published in 1988, 'The world unmoved' records Rankin. His first publisher, Bodley Head were going to drop him; he'd moved to London while Miranda his new wife supported his writing. Miranda Harvey (see where he got his pen name from folks) should not be underestimated in the development of Ian Rankin the author. Tremendously supportive, she allowed him to develop his craft where many wives would have suggested he got a proper job. They were living in Tottenham in North London and Rankin was commuting three hours a day to work for *Hi-Fi Review* magazine in South London (note the fancy turntable mentioned in *Hide and Seek*). He was also reviewing books for *Scotland on Sunday* whilst trying to write his own stuff. Around this time Rankin went on a writers' retreat and learnt the art of redrafting, so despite the lack of success in this period, he was honing his craft every day. Finally, he got around to writing *Hide and Seek* between all his other commitments.

Rankin notes how the events in the book mirrored a future real-life incident involving Edinburgh high society and rent boys. The scandal came to light eighteen months after the book was published and was known as the Magic Circle. It too involved suicide. A list of names was stolen from a police station. The investigating officers into the case were demoted back to uniform, it was all very fishy, with the parallels to this story like the idea of interfering with the course of justice strong. Rankin was starting to get lucky. Add to this a festering resentment of London's late 80's money-obsessed values and an increasing desire to chronicle a city he missed and loved and Rankin was starting to get his voice. This is still a fictional Edinburgh though; the Eyrie isn't real, Rebus still works at a made-up police station and the Pilmuir estate is a merging of two notorious estates in Edinburgh (Pilton and Muirhouse). What *is* real is that Edinburgh was perceived, certainly in the South of the UK as a heroin capital. It was almost a stereotypical problem with AIDS and dirty needles being as well-known and talked about as global warming is today, so this was almost certain to feature in a crime book in Edinburgh at the time. The sinkhole estates of Edinburgh were rarely mentioned in print but Rankin wanted to write about this, because no-one else was. The other London obsession with house prices also gets transferred to Edinburgh, as is Brian Holmes' sad description of his short time spent in London, which reads like Rankin telling us about his feelings.

23

Rankin couldn't quite let all his student affectations go, he referenced the Edinburgh university library on the fifth floor, where he used to work, added Rian, a character from his first novel *The Flood* as some weird (and never seen again) love interest for Rebus.

Things That Don't Make Sense:

There's something not quite right about the chronology of the Rebus series. And this is as good a place as any to lay the foundations. It's well-known that Rebus ages with the books, or, if you prefer, the books are in real time. Rankin wanted to avoid the eternally young James Bond and the Hercule Poirot effect where Poirot was retired in the first book in 1922 and still going fifty years later! This is fine, but Rebus is now a Detective Inspector and the text alludes to it being after a "long, hard case full of personal suffering". This *has* to be the *Knots and Crosses* case, which was in 1987 if we go by publishing dates. This book was published in 1991, four years after the events in *Knots and Crosses*. This is plausible, but the text also suggests that the promotion is recent, as he is delighted by how quickly a DI can get things done compared to a lowly DS. The most likely explanation is that Rankin hadn't given too much thought to the Rebus ageing process at this stage. There's certainly no ages or dates given, nor the slightest hint to it. Maybe Rebus had another case full of personal suffering that Rankin hasn't bothered to chronicle. The four-year gap remains problematic nevertheless.

While we're on the DI thing, would a DI have his own office? Rebus in the future certainly doesn't, and as mentioned before Superintendent Watson seems far more senior than he should be and where are the DCI's? We'll let Rankin off the police hierarchy research, he was working three jobs.

Calum McCallum, boyfriend of Gill Templer and famous DJ on the local Edinburgh radio station needs to get a better agent. He's working the late shift on Tuesday night then the breakfast show on Thursday morning. Don't star DJ's have one regular slot every day, the Breakfast show being the prime show? It certainly wouldn't be the late shift.

This should become a regular slot are the plot coincidences here a little too big? What are the chances of a randomly selected psychology lecturer just happening to know the very occultist student Rebus is looking for? What are the chances of Calum McAllum being involved with Gill Templer and also holding the key to Rebus's case as well? And while we're on it would the police really ignore the death of the junkie as implied here? It's pretty suspicious.

Rebus still has a lot of books.

And although Rankin points out the incongruity on a number of occasions it's still fair to ask whether you would spearhead an anti-drugs campaign with an officer with a borderline drink problem and a brother inside for drug dealing? We wouldn't neither. Oh and finally (and famously) Rankin describes the stones in the streets of Edinburgh as cobbles when they are known as setts. He'll get that right soon.

Musical references:

Apart from a brief mention of the Beatles' 'White' Album – nothing.

Review:

This is much better; from the opening scenes with a distracted Rebus at a dinner party, to the sordid underside of Edinburgh life we start to see Rankin finding his voice. Rebus really gets his teeth into this world and almost everything is in place; the scattershot approach to solving the case, his brilliant interview techniques, but also his emotional intelligence and genuine likeability. But crucially Rankin's writing is so much better now. Four years of honing your craft will do that for any writer and for one as good as Rankin, well...

It's a much tighter work, fitting better into the conventions, and Rankin is focused on the sort of book he is writing. He's not writing to order, but he knows what he's trying to do this time. He's losing his literary pretentions and finding his own voice in the Edinburgh world he will start to dominate.

There are still a few problems; the coincidences are a bit too much. The police procedure is still a little off. There is no team work at all and Rebus seems to be the only one doing anything, but the story rattles along and you barely notice at first read. It doesn't have the emotional bang of the later books, characters disappear without much explanation and we don't really care. Henchmen are plonked in at random, but there are some great moments too. The casino scene is wonderful, as the 'drunk Dundonians' try to get in, as is Rebus in the Eyrie. Less good are scenes where Rebus skews the perspective and we are inside the heads of two characters in one scene, which still allows us to be confused to whom we're supposed to be rooting for.

But Rebus is emerging, he knows a free mason's handshake when he feels it but hasn't yet learned to mimic them. And his anger at the end when he writes his resignation is lovely, but too rushed. We needed a little bit more than we get after the enormity of the story told here. The plot is very accomplished and occasional narrative voice slip-ups aside this is a good early Rebus book. This is where we start to see how good Rankin will become.

This is a great book to start the Rebus journey. It's not in the top ten but it's getting there and the seeds of one of the greatest detectives are being sewn.

Tooth and Nail

Published by: Century (Random house) 1992 and originally called *Wolfman*, see below.

One line Summary: Rebus is a fish out of water in 'the Smoke' on the trail of another serial killer, and this one has a lot more credibility.

Cover: The original *Wolfman* cover was a St Paul's cathedral – based painting of the London skyline with the Lady Justice statue from The Old Bailey courtrooms in the foreground, blindfolded and bloody. The reprint had a speeding London tube train, then we have some Hitchockian birds on telephone wires and finally Trafalgar Square.

TV adaptation: None.

Five Things to notice about Tooth and Nail:

1) Well it's obviously the one set in London. There are lots of reasons for this; especially that Rankin hadn't established the character of Edinburgh yet so putting Rebus in the place where he (Rankin) lived made sense. As this barely caused a ripple at the time, the move wasn't a big deal but reading it now it's a joyous exercise in seeing Rebus not fitting in, although quite how much Rankin was writing himself is another matter. He's done this before with Brian Holmes' memories of London but perhaps here is Rankin's angst really coming out.

2) If you had been one of the few who bought this book on the day of release then you would have actually bought a book called *Wolfman*. It was originally called

this until his American publishers felt it sounded too like something from the horror genre to work and suggested *Tooth and Nail* instead, which fitted in with the style of the previous two titles.

3) The London here is a strange mix of the real and the fictional, which although we didn't know it at the time, is to become a hallmark of the series. So the River Lea scenes in Tottenham are absolutely spot-on, as are the Old Bailey scenes. Other bits are totally made up; although Rankin is already so good it's hard to spot the join.

4) We've stolen this from the Things that don't Make Sense section but it's so blatant we've put it here. The truth is that it makes absolutely no sense for Rebus to called in by the Metropolitan Police at all. It's inferred in the text that the reason Rebus is invited down is because Rebus is some expert on serial killers, but is he? He was a lowly DS during the investigation and ignored most of the blatant clues that came his way. It makes no sense for the Metropolitan Police to call in someone like Rebus. Especially given the perceived know-it-all arrogance of the Met.

5) In interviews at this time in his career Rankin is already calling Rebus the big brother he never had. He's starting to like him.

First and Lasts:

If it had still been called *Wolfman* it would be the first of the series not to have the x and y title, but it isn't so it becomes the first book that doesn't play on a game for its title. It's the first and last time where not a single minute of the action takes place in Edinburgh but you'll have to wait and see if this is a good idea or not. This is also the first time we get to meet (or at least hear the name) Morris

Gerald Cafferty, although of course we don't meet him at all. And for the fruitier reader this is the last time we have to endure Rebus having sex and the act described in wayyy too much detail. First appearance of Doctor Curt - just the name, as an extended joke of thanks to mates at the back of the book. As we have seen Jon Curt was an old flat mate and part-time barman at the Oxford bar...

Now we have the boxing books out of the way, believe it or not the rugby reference here is the last reference to competitive sport (apart from football).

Finally it's the last blatant Jekyll and Hyde reference (thank God) although at least Rankin has the grace to joke about it.

Background:

This is well documented as Rankin's 'get London out of his system' book. He lived in London between 1986 and 1990 until Miranda decided they should move to France. Rankin's attitude was that he was suffering in London so why shouldn't Rebus? He records in his diary that in March 11th 1990 he had halfheartedly started *Wolfman.* He was hating the hi-fi journalism and claimed he had no idea what he was reviewing and couldn't believe the power he had, or that people actually read them.

Ah yes, *Wolfman* – the title. We've noted before how the serial killer was becoming en vogue and this time Rankin admits he was very taken with Thomas Harris's *The Silence of the Lambs* published in 1988 and widely available in paperback around the time when his ideas were coming together. The film is less likely to have been a source as it was released after the main drafts were written. One also gets the feeling that a Rankin (again) wants to rewrite his previous books and get it right, this time the serial killer material. The Harris influence meant the first draft was too graphic with regard to the sex and violence and his editor suggested cuts, although Rebus still gets fruity! There are lots of references to *Knots and Crosses*, which is unusual for the Rebus series, but logical

29

because the events of that book lead him to London. Rankin also notes that his father passed away in 1990 and he started to add more of his (and his father's) favourite Scottishisms into his prose. Here it is not quite so manifest but in the next book it will overflow.

The other thing that is well-known about this book is that Rankin did jury service while in London and he took copious notes at the time. The loophole that gets off one of the criminals happened while Rankin was there, although he claims the judge didn't notice.

What's also worth noting is how much more detail Rankin puts into his crime scene and autopsy scenes. He noted to himself that he needed to do more research and it's here on the page. In fact in contemporary interviews at the time the book was released he was keen to emphasise how important it is to get the detail right compared to Colin Dexter's Inspector Morse books (a common bugbear of his at the time). It's true he does get down to relating the boring detail of murder enquiries. He also reveals how he befriended a pathologist in Edinburgh although he avoided a real autopsy. When he was in Edinburgh he was starting to hear a lot of true stories from policemen in their pubs, one which was the Oxford Bar. This was a better approach than writing letters as he had before. In the same early interview Rankin was also deciding he wanted write about the problems in society today, which happens to involve a murder rather than the crossword puzzle approach to British novels at the time (and, dare we say it *Knots and Crosses*). He was nailing his colours to the American genre's mast, which were much more realistic.

The accuracy also goes for the London scenes. Rankin lived in a maisonette close to the river Lea in North London and the murder scene is accurately portrayed. Rankin describes how a few years later the word Wolfman was sprayed under a bridge nearby. It's a bit more gentrified now that Hackney is hipper and the Olympic stadium site is just downstream but the part where Rankin lived is still a little on the dodgy side... for those not familiar with North and East London the Hackney marshes on the other side of

30

the river Lea are where East-End Londoners go to play football on the weekend. It was immortalized in that classic Nike advert to Blur's *Parklife* - go look it up – now.

Things That Don't Make Sense:

Rebus travels south on the train on Sunday 18th March (year not given) after the rugby match between England and Scotland, which Scotland won 13-10. Hmmm... well, no match between Scotland and England has ended with this score but the game in 1990 ended with a 13-7 win to Scotland, and it was played on 17th March: note the diary entry date in the Background section said he had started the book at the start of that week. If this *is* the game he meant and he misremembered the score and wrote the scene on this day it throws further spanners into the Rebus dating thing, as this wasn't published until 1992! What makes even less sense from a rugby perspective is why DI Flight is watching the highlights 24 hours later (the game was shown live) and why English fans are returning home 24 hours after the game as it was over by mid-afternoon.

As we know, the historical accuracy was spot on for the river Lea killing scene but there sadly isn't a Wolf street, a Kilmore road, or a Gideon park off the Bow road.

Is anybody in London actually called Kenny? And did anybody ever say 'wotcha' outside of Chas and Dave songs?

Oh, and Rebus doesn't seem to use a boarding pass to go on the plane back to Glasgow. He seems to just use a ticket, and why does Rankin take the action up to Glasgow for five hours anyway? If it's just to get to a flea market he knows, then that's weird.

And what the hell is Rebus wearing?!

Musical references: Steppenwolf – Born to be wild – we wonder why?

31

Review:

The huge leaps in quality continue with the best of the 'early years' books and this is the first Rankin that deserves a place on the crime shelf. Rebus has fully evolved into the character we know and love, although his dress sense isn't right. And for the first time Rankin delivers plot-wise. This is logical, coherent and the clues are there but well disguised, with no cheating (ok, a little bit of cheating with the voice of the Wolfman being a tad contrived and over-disguised, but it works for the character). This is the third attempt by Rankin to start this series and indeed this has all the things *Knots and Crosses* didn't have; solid police procedure, nice clues, bit of gore but also improves on the plotting of *Hide and Seek*. The teeth marks, for example is a great idea. Even the increased research and realism just works, although a lot of writers have caught up in 2015 so its power has lessened over time. This is also the problem with the serial killer plot line. Such killers in fiction are ten-a-penny now, and this reads a little clichéd to a modern eye, which isn't Rankin's fault at all.

There are other flaws: stylistically Rankin still shifts the narrative point of view mid-scene, which leads to the weird scene where Rebus meets Sammy's boyfriend Kenny, and the point of view switches from Rebus to Kenny almost mid-sentence. It's effective but it would have been better entirely through Rebus's eyes and would have worked just as well. Proof readers call it 'Head Hopping' and is usually frowned upon, but it does pop up occasionally in Rankin's books. The other problem is that this didn't need to be set in London at all, which is a shame, as this is the unique selling point. It could have worked just as well in another part of Scotland, or even Edinburgh. This is the real nub of the problem for this as part of a series. We, the readers don't know Rebus well enough yet, so the idea of taking Rebus out of Edinburgh and making him a fish out of water doesn't work because the series' essential 'Edinburghness' has yet to be consolidated.

So it's great, with lots of one liners and great Rebus moments, but it's way too early to take him away from Edinburgh and so it is toothless (ironically) and it's no surprise the experiment hasn't really been repeated since. This is great as a stand-alone or as part of a series, just needed to be ten books further down the line.

A Good Hanging and Other Stories

Published by: Century 1992

Cover: A painting with a quite literal interpretation of a noose in chocolate box style. The loop of the noose encircles Edinburgh Castle. The reprint has a gloomy staircase with a human silhouette in the background.

Firsts and Lasts:

This is the first of three short story compilations. The other firsts will be dealt with below.

Background:

Rankin has always been a fan of the short story and wrote short them continuously, often to break writers' block, others for short-story compilations and competitions. Entering competitions is another fine way to hone the craft of the writer. This compilation covered the early years. This has the feel of a stop gap compilation but as it is on a new publishing house, it's harder to be sure why it was published.

In the introduction to his 'definitive' short story collection *The Beat Goes On* in 2014 Rankin revealed that each of these stories is supposed to take place on continuous months of a year, with the first taking place in April and the last in December. There's no evidence in the book as published for this and he had never mentioned this before, although it makes a lot of sense. In truth, many of the stories here have no discernible dates so we debate whether this idea was written with this in mind and is more of a loose fit. *Playback* for example was definitely published in 1990 and so not part of this masterplan.

The stories:

Playback (This story first appeared in the Winter's Crimes Collection, No. 22, published in 1990)

The Eyrie is mentioned and Holmes gets a chance to pun, which suggests 1990ish. This is a clever little tale with a nice denouement, although it's written early enough to not have Rankin's sociological research in place. The half an hour death window is a little unlikely, for example. Rebus seems genuinely confused by answer phone technology. The dénouement is probably a little obvious to anyone who's into crime fiction. Some argue this is named after the Philip Marlowe story – the one that was never filmed - but it's more likely to be a coincidence.

The Dean Curse

It's difficult to work out when this one was written, as Farmer Watson is only a Superintendent, not the Chief Superintendent he is in the previous book. Rebus is seen giving up on Dashiell Hammett book *The Dain Curse* from 1929 and throwing it in the air, bemoaning the coincidences, oh the irony. This isn't too bad, another twisty one but better disguised than the first story. At least Rebus does some good detective work. And there's nothing better than Rebus brushing up against stiff military types. This story seems very popular with the hardcore detective fiction fans, those who think Rankin is usually a little plodding and Victorian in his need to discuss Edinburgh and Scottish life as well.

Being Frank

A whimsical tale about Frank the tramp that makes the idea of vagrancy seem romantic for a moment. Mrs. Cochrane makes an appearance but this is so heavy on coincidence as to be annoying. Another early tale if the jazz is anything to go by.

Concrete Evidence

Doctor Curt's first appearance dates this to definitely after *Tooth and Nail*, and more likely during the writing of *Strip Jack*. This gives us the knowledge that Rebus supported Hearts as a kid in 1960, and was trying to lose his virginity. I make it he was 13 then - randy sod. Aside from that this is a good early attempt at what he got a lot better at in *Set in Darkness,* where a body is found in a cellar of the Parliament. Aside from that we have a lot of wine knowledge suddenly. Does this coincide with Rankin's move to France? There's also our first Rolling Stones reference as he mouths the words to *Yesterday's Papers*. This is the most satisfying by far of the short stories here, and nearly of all the early stories.

Seeing Things

In which Rankin reinvents John Rebus from the Bible quoting, almost firebrand of *Knots and Crosses* and turns him into a Christian who has too many doubts to ally himself to either Catholic or Protestant. It's interesting that a man who will later claim to have Polish routes isn't Catholic although Rebus argues that it was his mother who was the religious one, and a Protestant. Also, as the last story noted Rebus *did* support the Protestant team in Edinburgh. This is post *Tooth and Nail*, as he calls his old mate George Flight. Aside from this we have a fun little tale about celestial visions and cocaine and Rankin even lets us have a cute ending, even if the murder itself is utterly unlikely. Oh, and is Rebus left-handed? He claims to kick a football with his left foot.

A Good Hanging

Rebus investigates a hanging of an actor during the Edinburgh festival. Seasoned crime novel writers will get worried at this point because a murder of an actor that is dressed up to look like an accident with a prop (here, a gallows, there a fake knife) at the Edinburgh festival was done by Simon Brett in *So Much Blood*, a Charles Paris mystery in 1977. We even have similar acronyms for the players: 'ART' and 'DUDS'; both of whom perform Shakespeare plays and both stories are named after Shakespeare quotes: 'so much blood' from *Macbeth*, 'a good hanging' from *Twelfth Night*. And, although we have absolutely no doubt that Rankin had never read Simon Brett (he has always claimed to detest Morse-like cosiness and, good Lord the Charles Paris books are like a pair of slippers on a cold day) anyone writing about a murder in a troupe of student actors at Edinburgh is going to write about the same types. Of course Rankin will revisit the festival properly in *Mortal Causes*. The quote itself (which is also the title – but not completed) - does indeed lead to the solution...

This was written before *Tooth and Nail*, as Professor Curt isn't named, Brian Holmes is gloomy and Rebus is very good at remembering Shakespeare, oh yes this is early, and a bit lame.

Tit for Tat

Rebus investigates a fire in a tenement. This reeks of a story heard in the Oxford bar, told by an ex-policeman. The set-up is nice and we have cracking Rankinian lines but this fizzles away to nothing, sinking in its own implausibility. Quite likeable though, nevertheless.

Not Provan

We liked this one. Rebus is often at his best in the real shitty parts of town and this one has a lot of that. It plays on a football technicality that wouldn't work because the police appear not to know about this, yet they would absolutely have known because they would have made the call. Read the story and you'll see what we mean. There's not enough here really to make it stand out, but pleasantly Rebusy.

Sunday

Another early tale dated by the references to Frank of 'being Frank' fame, Holmes relationship with Nell, bookish Rebus and more jazz. This looks like being in the style of the classic Tony Hancock half hour radio comedy *Sunday afternoon at Home* until the twist at the end and instead we get an absolute gem of understated character development that's worth the entry fee alone.

Auld Lang Syne

Rebus and Hogmanay has never been explored and this tale of drug dealing at midnight works well. Rab Philips from *Seeing Things* is mentioned and we learn that Rebus is still au fait with Masonic handshakes, but the writing obscures if this is the first reference to him being able to return them. We also learn that Rebus does believe is coincidence: I'm not surprised! Also the only time Fart Lauderdale is known as 'the clockwork orange man'. The nickname will be reassigned very soon. This can be reasonably dated to around 1990 based on a criminal who was put away by Rebus still thinking he was a sergeant. It has a nice twist, but there was probably a better story here than the one told: one with just a little bit of hope - oh well.

The Gentlemen's Club

Even darker than the story above this tale of teenage suicide could work as a whole novel and Rebus has to have two rather extraordinary flashes of inspiration to get to the solution inside the word count. Rebus is still very knowledgeable about Shakespeare

Monstrous Trumpet

Inspector Cluzeau from Perigueux (which is where Rankin lived in France) takes the lead, as Rankin writes what he knows. Lots of cultural clashes and pochette jokes but little to keep us here except to date it by the Professor Curt reference and to clearly living in France to after *Tooth and Nail*, and note the first time we see Rankin's recurring interest in fine art appear in a story.

Verdict:

Short story compilations are like albums: the placing of the tracks is as vital as the positioning of these stories. A great couple of openers and hide the filler in the middle. The order isn't right here.

If you're new to the books you have 19 proper novels to catch up with first so go there. If you're a Rebus fan, this is awesome. Although none of the tales here ultimately amount to much we see the Rebus character emerging on every page. The TV series would have been far better of serializing these than attempting and bastardising the proper novels. This is a vital read for the true fan.

Strip Jack

Published by: Orion (1992)

One line summary: Rebus is on hand when a popular politician is caught in a sting on a brothel. As the man's life unravels Rebus gets involved in the unpicking.

Cover: The original is the only one Rankin had involvement in. The British Houses of Parliament, with a formal Scottish flag flying over an orange sunset. Every other edition has gone for moody pictures of buildings.

TV adaptation: Second Ken Stott season, third episode. Most notable for turning Gregor Jack from a politician to a millionaire with a social conscience! It was also dramatized for BBC Radio 4 starring Ron Donachie (Ser Rodrik Cassel from *Game of Thrones)* in 2010.

Four things to notice about Strip Jack:

1. Well it's another relaunch in our opinion, and we cite the huge number of introductions in the First and Last section. This is where you can see Rankin start to think about the Rebus universe and putting things in place that will be the touchstones for his books. So we get a girlfriend, a sidekick, a bad boss, and he starts to use the real Edinburgh where he can. Rankin is hot on realism, which is ironic in this story, as we'll see.

2. Paronomasia: the fancy word for the pun. It is worth noting at this point that Rankin likes a pun, but this is the first time they become a trope. In fact the most noticeable thing about this book is the light tone, there are jokes and quips as well as puns and it's really rather odd if you come at this

from reading the later books. Rankin clearly has a playful sense of humour and you can feel him testing the water here. It's an experiment that won't last, even if the worst pun of the series is yet to come...

3. There is a case for this being the second time that Rebus is killed off, in the Reichenbach falls moment at the end of the book. Rankin pulls back but did he mean it?

4. The Rebus books have been published as audio books. The original reader was Bill Paterson, but he dropped out, see *Black and Blue* for the reason why. James Macpherson, a reasonably well-known actor who had appeared in Taggart took over and did a great job. According to Rankin he won an award for his reading of the audio version of *Strip Jack*.

First and lasts:

First time Rankin puts quotes at the front of a book: from George Bernard Shaw and Libanus in this case. First appearance of the following important characters: Patience Aitken, Rebus's main squeeze for the next few books; DCI Frank 'fart' Lauderdale, who is presented as someone who we should know about already, actually so is Patience. OK, OK Lauderdale appeared in a short story in *A Good Hanging*... but this is his real debut. Also, Doctor Curt makes his first appearance (although again this will depend on when Rankin actually wrote the short story *Concrete Evidence*) – yes, the nit pickers will point out the reference at the back of *Tooth and Nail*, but that was just a joke, not a character. This could be the first appearance of Rebus's iconic Saab 900, but it isn't. The last appearance of Rebus's muttered 'fytp' to annoying people, last time we go to the fictional Great London Road police station and Rankin guarantees we'll never be back, but we also get the first mention of the St Leonard's station, even if we don't go there. It's also the first time we see Farmer Watson's coffee machine. It's the last story title based on a game, although only partially, strip jack naked being a

41

less well-known name for beggar my neighbour. If you prefer, it's the first time an x and y title hasn't been used. Oh, and perhaps most important of all, this is the first Rankin book to be published by Orion, a new publishing group who really got behind Rankin. Their support is as crucial to the story as Rankin's writing. First proper Rolling Stones reference, after the brief nod to *Yesterday's Papers* in *A Good Hanging...*

This is the only time Rankin got involved with the cover design on the original hardback, a lion attacking the Westminster parliament building. Oh, and the first mention of the Oxford bar, although it's in the acknowledgements, so it doesn't count.

Background:

In the early 1990's Rankin and his wife moved to a tumbledown house in Périgord in the Dordogne region of South west France. Rankin spent a lot of time doing up the farmhouse, and was also writing the Jack Harvey novels as well, to supplement his income, or hedge his bets. In his own words, his writing wasn't really paying; he reckons he was earning £5000 a year at this stage ($8000) But as anyone will tell you who has lived abroad and doesn't have a great grasp on the language, you start to miss home, and become excessively patriotic. You look to home when you're far away, which might help explain why *Strip Jack* is classified by many critics and Rankin himself, as his most Scottish work, ostensibly because he starts to really crank up the Scottish-isms. *Strip Jack's* Scottishness is a symptom, nothing more. But we would also argue that this increase in Scottishness is down to being monolingual in a foreign country. You go into your shell a lot when you can't follow conversations. This book was inevitable.

Rankin also felt that as he was now a full-time writer he ought to get the details right and made further contact with Edinburgh pathologist Professor Busuttil to give his autopsy scenes realism. Rankin would also go to Edinburgh three or four times a year to get the flavour of place, take pictures and beg sofas to sleep on. It's also clear (also noted in *A Good Hanging* preceding this) that Rebus's memories are increasingly Rankin's memories. For example Rankin attributes the glorious 'Suey' nickname used here to a real friend of his from school.

So this is the book where Rankin felt his apprenticeship ends and he became a full-time writer. The fictional world is gone, made-up Old London Road is burnt down and now he knows he's writing a series he gets his support cast right. Farmer Watson is back and much more Presbyterian. Fart Lauderdale is in to give us a bad boss, the old nickname gone after the experiment in *A Good Hanging*. Rebus gets a girlfriend in Patience Aitken, who takes nominative determinism to new levels. She lives at Oxford Terrace, where a mate of Rankin lived, who is later rewarded with a cameo in the Sutherland bar.

Finally, it has to be said that this is the lightest and most deliberately humorous of the books so far. Notice we didn't say 'funny', the puns are excruciating and the lightness is almost the last of the Rankin stylistic experiments.

Things That Don't Make Sense:

This book was repackaged into the 'St Leonard's Years' omnibus collection, when it isn't set in St Leonard's.

You have to admire a man who started as a crime writer then admitted he didn't know much about police procedure. We mention this because he's about to do the same thing here, writing a political novel without knowing much about politics! We can excuse *Knots and Crosses* because Rankin didn't mean to be writing crime fiction, but here you have the same author writing about the British Parliamentary system. First of all, as Rankin admits the seat of North and South Esk is fictional; in the acknowledgements he points out the geographical area is sort of Midlothian, with a bit of Edinburgh Pentlands prior to the 1983 boundary commission changes. He also thanks Alex Eadie, MP for Midlothian. All fine, on balance so moving on... the first thing that makes little sense is for Gregor Jack to be an Independent MP. When the book was written there hadn't been a genuine independent MP in the mainland UK for about 50 years. The six technically independent MP's had been affiliated to major parties. For example Dick Taverne was deselected as the MP for Lincoln by the Labour Party in his region for his lack of support for the joining of the Common Market. He then formed his own democratic Labour Party, stood and won. This was in 1974 and there wasn't another one until Martin Bell, a genuine independent was elected MP for Tatton in 1997. This was a weird case, as he stood against Neil Hamilton, a Conservative MP mired in sleaze allegations. He stood and the Liberal Democrat and Labour Party withdrew their candidates to give him a free run. So, essentially there's no way Jack would be independent. Nobody who goes into politics doesn't join a political party. A political party funds MPs, their publicity machines and various other perks, without which it would be impossible to operate. Secondly, Jack finds there is pressure on him to resign? From whom? He's not a minister, so he does not answer to the Prime Minister, or the leader of the opposition. As he's independent he does not have to answer to a constituency committee, who could deselect him. He answers to no-one. Thirdly, a politician cannot simply resign anyway, as suggested in the book. In fact it is theoretically forbidden to resign. To get around it a fiction (one which Rankin would love) exists where Members of Parliament wishing to give up their seats are commonly appointed by the Chancellor of the Exchequer to an office which has the possibility of a payment from the Crown. A number of offices have been used for this purpose historically, but only two are provided for in present legislation. The two offices, which currently allow Members to vacate their seats, are as follows: Crown Steward and Bailiff of the three Chiltern Hundreds of Stoke, Desborough and Burnham, or a similar role related to the Manor of Northstead. The offices are only nominally paid. Generally they are vacant until they are needed again to effect the resignation of an MP. The Chiltern Hundreds is usually used alternately with the Manor of Northstead, which makes it possible for two members to resign at the same time. So Gregor Jack is a bit of a problem, mainly because Rankin misunderstood the machinations of politics. How hard would it have been for Rankin to make Jack a Labour MP, or even hipper, SNP?

In one chapter Rebus says he went to school in Cowdenbeath but in *Dead Souls* we'll find this corrected to Auchteruddan. Oops. What's even weirder is that this is one of those mistakes that Rankin happily acknowledges in interviews and in print. In his book *Rebus's Scotland* he admits the mistake – but the thing is, he thinks he makes the mistake in *The Black Book*, which is true, but he forgot he mentions it earlier here too! Double oops.

Rebus is also a bit too keen on football here. Perhaps Italia 90 got to him.

Oh, and no DI from Edinburgh would go haring off to the Highlands like Rebus does. They'd call their colleagues in the area to do the dirty work. But that would be boring.

We're not convinced that Rebus would undertake self-hypnosis to help with his anxiety. Rankin was doing so at the time but it doesn't feel right for Rebus, despite the hypnosis background in the family.

Finally, the plot hinges on the colour of a car that was either blue, or green. Surely nobody would mix up such colours?

Musical references:

Two Rolling Stones references: *Let it Bleed* and *Paint it Black*. Rebus also mentions the Stones when he mentions the Beatles' *Sergeant Pepper*, saying second best is OK if you can't get the Stones. Brief references to Simple Minds, Fleetwood Mac and Eric Clapton, as well as some opera.

Review:

This is a tough one to review. Even Rankin calls it the book that ends his apprenticeship: the inference being that he's still not found his voice. That is certainly true, and *Knots* aside, this is the weakest of the series. The major problem is that the tone is far too light, almost jaunty in places. The puns, a recent affectation, are excruciating, and just wrong in many ways. There's a lightness and an almost new laddish jocularity here, which was fashionable at the time but doesn't work for Rebus. Add to this that Gregor Jack as a character isn't drawn well enough. He should hold the book in his thrall. This is a man who is an MP without any political party back-up. He should be a superstar, yet he doesn't come across like that. He comes across as pathetic and weak. He wouldn't be, he couldn't be. Rankin will fail to pull off the same trick with the similarly charismatic Aengus Gibson in the next book.

But Rankin knows where he wants to be, he just hasn't found the pulse yet and until he finds it he can't get to the heart of Edinburgh. Tonally this might be a mis-step but this is the first time we get a nicely entwined plot line with good character, motivation, some clever misdirection and good police work. Rankin is doing his research and it's paying off. He's losing the fictional baggage and clearing the decks to focus on what's needed. He just needs to lose the chatty voice.

The Black Book

Published by: Orion (1993)

One line summary: All roads lead to 'Big Ger' Cafferty, as the titular black book provides clues to some murders. Oh, and the series gets some balls.

Cover: The original had an embossed black cover with black writing interspersed with various flames. Follow-ups include one with a fallen down wooden fence, some scaffolding and some trees.

TV adaptation: Well there was an episode called *The Black Book* but it had nothing to do with this story! It was the first episode of Ken Stott's second season. The radio adaptation was in 2012.

Two things to notice about The Black Book (but they're two very big things):

1) We'll mention this in the Firsts and Lasts section but of course this is the first time Rebus meets DC Siobhan Clarke, who will become a major character in these books. It's difficult to know if Rankin had any idea what he was creating, she's just another DC at St Leonard's. However within a few short appearances she's more appealing and more popular than the assigned side-kick Brian Holmes.

2) And while we're at it this is the first time Maurice Gerald Cafferty's evil tendrils start to make their mark. We'll talk quite a lot about him of course, but for the early fan who read all of Rankin's books in order this sudden appearance of a Moriarty figure for Rebus must have come as a bit of a shock.

First and lasts:

Deep breath, there's a lot.

If we're being bitchy this is the first Rebus book with a really boring title. Ok, ok it's the first story that has neither a game, nor an xxxx and xxx title. It's the only book to have references to *all* the previous books.

It's the first book where Rebus doesn't get any sex, the first appearance of St Leonard's station proper, first appearance of Siobhan Clarke, the first almost direct follow up story, in that Rebus still suffering from the burns in *Strip Jack*. Big Ger Cafferty makes his proper debut too, as does his Strawman nickname for Rebus. First appearance of Mairie Henderson, who will be the investigative journalist we love for quite a few books. The Fourth estate gets short shrift in these books usually but Mairie is great and we get the impression that Rankin is rather fond of her too. He gets us (and most of the male characters) to fall in love with her without much of a physical description, aside from her legs. Oh, and it's implied we know her. First actual mention of the name Arden Street as where Rebus lives.

Nearly there, first appearance of the patriotic organization the Sword and Shield. First use of the C bomb, but in a very Malcolm Tucker way. First mention of Father Conor Leary, the Catholic priest Rebus uses to check his faith, although he's not named yet. Last mention of the Sutherland bar. And although this isn't a first or last, Jack Morton is back!

Oh and the first and last time Rebus is, sort of off the cigarettes.

Background:

In 1991 Ian Rankin and Miranda had been living in France for a year. Rankin was getting into a zone of writing two books a year:

48

now settled as a Rebus book and a Jack Harvey thriller. That summer he won the Raymond Chandler Fulbright award, which consisted of a paid for six-month stay in the USA. This was obviously very exciting, but coincided almost exactly with Mrs. Rankin becoming pregnant. Interviews with Rankin at the time, he was promoting *Tooth and Nail*, made mention of his dilemma about taking a baby to America, but take a baby is what they did. They spent a month in Seattle and five months on the road in a VW camper van and the experience affected Rankin in a number of ways. Firstly he was certain he was writing a series now and decided to toughen up the realism. Out would go the fictional aspects, in would come more real locations, although he is doing himself down slightly here, as St Leonard's was heavily foreshadowed in *Strip Jack*. And pubs like the Hawes inn in Queensferry are real locations. Secondly, it gave Rankin the idea for the Elvis themed restaurant (fictional) in Edinburgh. He saw one like it in Louisiana. Rankin would have appreciated the puns on the menu, he does love a pun and perhaps this gave him too many excuses to create excruciating ones for his fictional menu. Thirdly, we get another and almost final lurch in writing style. He had devoured a lot of American crime fiction and this results in the slightly too American-noir start.

The last piece in the decision to make this a series also allows a foil in Cafferty to appear, as well as a proper side-kick in Siobhan Clarke to muscle her was into the story. In a few scenes, she manages to almost totally write out dear old Brian Holmes. Rankin's other 'economy' was that a series allowed him to reuse old characters rather than constantly create new ones, which explains the reappearance of Vanderhyde, Jack Morton, Michael Rebus and most importantly Cafferty, although see Things that Don't Make Sense.

The Cafferty appearance is important of course. Rankin's official line is that this is his take on *Confessions of a Justified Sinner*, an 1824 work by James Hogg that became very popular in the latter part of the 20th Century. As it is set in Edinburgh and features a first person narrative of an antihero - let's put it this way, it's right up Rankin's street. The more obvious source and one that Rankin has acknowledged in print is Lawrence Block's Matt Scudder books, where our hero befriends a notorious gangster. Scudder has a complicated relationship with a hood called Mick Ballou, and you can see the Rebus/Cafferty relationship reflecting that here. This is a much better source, though perhaps less pretentious.

Rankin says: Cafferty's an amalgam of several real-life Glasgow 'gangsters'. I've definitely read accounts of how such real-life '60s villains as Jimmy Boyle made the trip to London and did strong-arm work for the likes of the Krays and the Richardsons. This may have been mentioned in Boyle's own autobiography, or in one of the many true crime books written about the Glasgow underworld... I definitely came across the info somewhere. One of these days I'm going to write a short story – maybe a long story – about Cafferty's early years." Never happened of course.

Rankin's regular research trips to Edinburgh reminded him of the smell of the Brewery and he also noted the suspicious rumours of a hotel fire mentioned by the off duty policemen in the Oxford bar - where he really spent his time researching.

"So there was a learning process going on, but it became a lot easier when cops came up to me and said, 'I loved the books...', because I would say, 'What's your phone number?' and I would start pestering them for information, and it's got to the stage now where the police in Scotland are very friendly to me. They understand that Rebus is a maverick but they like the fact that this guy doesn't follow the rules all of the time."

Things That Don't Make Sense:

There's the usual and inevitable list here of errors because of Rankin's shift in emphasis, but we'll start with the hilarious idea that a man of Rebus's generation would go get a massage in any circumstances, especially off a fella. And call us snobs but we think Rankin makes a big assumption that his readers know where and what the Bowery is and what its reputation was like.

As ever Rankin pretends to 'do sport' but clearly doesn't. Here, it's difficult to pin the Aberdeen v Hibernian result down. Hibernian definitely lost to Aberdeen in 1993 but it was in November and drew 0-0 at home after, but Siobhan notes it's nowhere near Christmas in the book!! Hibernian also lost after the book was published in the league. Best choice is probably the Cup match in April 1993 except for the 2-2 draw afterwards, which doesn't fit. And Rebus is back being vague about his football knowledge, after being quite the expert in *Strip Jack*. He doesn't know the name of Aberdeen's stadium here, and he would. Shall we stop trying?

The whole Cafferty thing is a bit confusing. As we've noted, Cafferty is mentioned off-screen in *Tooth and Nail* but here he has exploded into a huge Hyde to Rebus's Jekyll, and it's hard to justify. If Cafferty was this man who Rebus clearly detests surely he would have been mentioned more than a brief nod in one book? Also, the Strawman nickname story is glorious and it seems to date from the court case in *Tooth and Nail*, but it was never mentioned in that book. It seems too good an anecdote to have missed if Cafferty is who he is supposed to be. It sounds like a policeman anecdote from the Oxford Bar.

Rebus here again claims he was schooled in Cowdenbeath. Oh, and the black book is virtually irrelevant.

Musical References:

A lot, and that's even if we discard the awful Elvis puns at the diner. We can, at this point assume there will be Rolling Stones references, but we get our only Patsy Cline, but also Mary Hopkin gets a name check, as do early Pink Floyd, kd lang, The Jesus and Mary Chain, and the Doors.

51

Review:

By a mile the best Rebus yet. Thanks to the Fulbright award, there is an American twang to the style, more monologue, although it must be said the book takes an age to go anywhere. The unresolved Nell twist is great, as is the Patience line, although we have no real feel for her. The plot meanders and loops but holds together. We could have done with more Black Aengus too. Siobhan in her first appearance makes a great cop. It's true it starts too American and drifty and the puns still need to go, but this is weighty and well worth your time.

Rankin has grown in confidence and thrown his arms open wide. We now are close to having a master story teller. Cafferty is never more evil than here and it's easy to forget what a piece of work he is with his more legit persona of later books. It's a credit to Rankin that Cafferty feels well-established and drawn, yet we've never met him. Then, contrast this with the masterstroke of the anonymous, deliberate and gender-free description of Rebus's student tenants, which works despite the idea sounding ludicrous when written down here. He even has the confidence to take Rebus back to his own home town of Cardenden.

In many ways this is the Rubicon moment. We cross from a fictional, vaguely drawn world to a real character in a real city with a beating heart. There are still a few stylistic problems which Rankin himself seems to iron out as the book progresses, but there are lots of great scenes including our favourite: Rebus having a massage!! But also the tremendous colour of the Broadsword bar clientele; at last Rebus has his voice.

Mortal Causes

Published by: Orion 1994

One line summary: When a body is found murdered using a typical IRA technique Rebus takes on the religious division in Scotland.

Cover: A silhouette looks at Edinburgh castle as a giant pair of eyes look down from the sky. The reprint went for the famously irrelevant round tower. Late editions went for a sinister butcher's hook.

TV adaptation: The was last John Hannah story filmed in 2001 but not actually shown for a few years because its terrorist theme and its planned release date were too close the 9/11 atrocity.

Four things to notice about Mortal Causes:

1) It contains one of Rankin's favourite one liners: Rebus is asked if he has any enemies and replies: "I can think of half a dozen who would throw confetti at my funeral." It's good, but we still prefer Basque Separatists in *The Naming of the Dead*.

2) It's also the first of many of Rankin's books with a death reference in the title, *Dead Souls, Naming of the Dead* etc. will follow. Rankin has been quoted as saying there is a shadow of death over his family; his father and mother had both been married before and both spouses had died. Sadly his mother died in her 50s when Rankin was 18, his father too died relatively young.

3) Professor Curt drives a Saab, Gregor Jack drives a Saab. Rebus's car is yet to be named, but it's a Saab. Rankin is fascinated by Saabs. Anyone know why? Talking of Curt, he has reeled in his puns since his last outing and just gives

us his comedy, 'well he's dead' line on seeing the corpse – which is glorious, by the way.

4) And talking of puns. This is the high/low point of the series. The Queensferry rules one is one of the best but the 'Now Hans that does dishes can feel as soft as Gervase with mild, green, hairy-lipped squid' is just unforgivable. Ian, Ian drop the puns!

Firsts and lasts:

First appearance of Cafferty's grotesque henchman the Weasel and the first appearances of DS Claverhouse and DC Ormiston, who will annoy Rebus for a few books (although see Things that Don't Make Sense). You can make an argument for this being the first of the punning titles that will dominate the first part of the 21st Century.

Last mention of the fictional Eyrie restaurant, where the highfliers go to dine, and last mention of actor Rab Kinnoul from *Strip Jack*. First (brief) appearance of DI Shug Davidson of Torpichen station, who'll be around for a long time. First mention of Siobhan's vegetarianism and the first use of the word SOCO (Like CSI) as an acronym.

The sinkhole and entirely fictional Pilmuir Estate makes its last appearance, and if you don't count *Tooth and Nail*, which was set in London, this is the only book without a scene at Arden street.

And finally the Oxford bar makes its first appearance as just some bar.

Background:

This is set several months after *The Black Book* and Rankin struggled with the title for a change. Eventually Miranda gave him the idea. This one works beautifully, Rankin (of course) liking the pun of 'mortal', which can mean very drunk in Scottish, like a lot of things can.

You get the feeling Rankin was itching to write about 'the troubles', Miranda was from Northern Ireland so he had a lot of experience to draw on. Although Scotland has sectarian issues, just read anything about the two Glasgow football clubs, it clearly isn't as ideologically divided as Northern Ireland is/was, but it would have been there in any Scottish upbringing. Rankin writes of his own experiences in Fife and gives them to Rebus. He added realism as usual; the loyalist Alan Fowler is loosely based on real loyalist Billy Wright. And of course Rebus, a good soldier, would have served in Northern Ireland (although the timing is a little tight) and he recognizes an IRA punishment when he sees one.

Adding the Edinburgh Fringe Festival setting would have made sense now that Edinburgh, the city is almost a character of her own. One of Rankin's 'research' visits to Edinburgh (where he slept on friends' sofas and drank at the Ox) coincided with the Festival, presumably the 1993 one.

The other driving force in the narrative was Rankin's discovery of the Lawrence Bloch's Matt Scudder books. We've mentioned them before in the development of Cafferty, but here the hero, an alcoholic ex-cop, now private detective bleeds into Rebus too. So influential is Bloch that in the next book Rebus's drinking comes to the fore and he almost acts as a private detective rather than a conventional policeman.

Ten years after publication the six-pack shooting at the start of this book caused a little literary stir between Rankin and Val McDermid. It was a storm in a tea cup brought on by Rankin being very generous with his time and happy to give lots of interviews. In 2006 in an interview in *The Independent* he got caught out discussing the depiction of violence in books.

"Unlike rivals such as Patricia Cornwell, Karin Slaughter and Mo Hayder, he does not salivate over every drop of blood. 'The people writing the most graphic violence today are women,' he says when I ask what he thinks of them. 'If you turn that off,' he looks nervously at my tape recorder, but continues regardless, going public about one of the great unsaids among crime writers, 'I will tell you that they are mostly lesbians as well, which I find interesting.' He refuses to go into more detail. When I recall one book in which a woman was brutally raped and murdered, he flinches. 'Most male crime writers I know would flinch morally from over-describing an act of violence against a woman, a rape, murder or whatever.' Would he ban it? 'When they did a study of killers in the States, they found the books they had all read were the Bible and Catcher in the Rye.' His voice drips sarcasm. 'Should we ban them? No.'

A year later McDermid, at the Edinburgh books festival, attacked Rankin. McDermid, rejected Rankin's remarks as, "arrant rubbish." She went on to say, "I find that statement so offensive, I can't even begin to start. Apart from the fact that a lot of what is being written by the very talented young Scottish male writers is not shying away from depicting violence very directly."

McDermid then went to Rankin's books to find an example of violence in his books and criticized the "chilling" opening to *Mortal Causes*. Looking back it was all a bit of nonsense and Rankin should have kept his mouth shut, but choosing that scene isn't particularly clever, as the act of violence is not particularly dwelt upon. The truth is there are two types of crime writers: those who are in it for the horror and those who are in it for the crime. Rankin has never been about the gore, but many people love books where gore and violence are at the forefront. You pay your money and take your choice. There's a whole library of different styles within the genre.

Things That Don't Make Sense:

Although Rankin provides a get-out clause by clearly stating that this is all set in a fictional 1993 'before the Shankhill Road bombing and its bloody aftermath' he *is* writing about what he knows again because the mentioned football match and festival *did* occur at the same time, just the wrong year. On 22nd August 1992 (during the festival) Hearts did play Hibernian, but this was written after the 1993 festival when Rankin had been in town researching away from France and seeing a bit of the festival. By the way, in 1993 Hibernian didn't play Hearts until January, and drew, unlike the loss Father Leary implies here. As is often the case Rankin is nearly prescient, because Hibs *did* play Hearts in the year of publication (1994) when the festival was on, but the result is the wrong way round.

A convicted murderer and one of the UK's most dangerous men (Cafferty) escapes from Barlinnie prison and nobody seems to care? A bunch of teenage reprobates from a sink-hole estate attack the centre of Edinburgh tooled up with machine guns meant for the UDF and this isn't a big deal? This would be major news right across the UK, probably the world!

In the preparation stages of this book we considered adding a 'ridiculous coincidences' section but vetoed it is as a trivial piece of smart-arsedness our part. However, here the coincidence that the priest Rebus visits almost randomly from *The Black Book* is worried about the youth club leader on an estate that just happens to be the hub of a major arms theft operation is a little too much.

Ormiston gets promoted from a DC when we first meet him to a DS the next time we meet him about 30 pages later. That's fast promotion, or the first of the many DC/DS errors in the next few books.

Rebus feels he should know what SandS stands for. How long ago was *The Black Book*? It takes him 105 pages to remember.

DI Flower is given the nickname the Clockwork Orangeman by Rebus here. That's funny, because it was the nickname Rebus gave DI Lauderdale in *A Good Hanging and other stories*!

How hard would it be to spot an IRA six pack killing?

Musical References:

Firstly, the quote at the start – from Tom Waits, then we have Rolling Stones (no really!), Jethro Tull (he's a fan), Sex Pistols, Led Zeppelin, Simple Minds, Tie a Yellow Ribbon round the old oak tree - Tony Orlando and Dawn (yuk), Nico and Velvet Underground, Chet Baker, the Skye Boat Song (a Scottish standard) and Small Town Saturday Night by Hal Ketchum.

Review:

Throughout this series so far we've been looking for Rankin to finally deliver a blinder and this...isn't quite there...but it's so very close, because he quite literally loses the plot. In its favour it's one of Rankin's least coincidence-heavy books, Rebus, as a character is absolutely crystal clear and beautifully drawn. Rankin's other character, the city of Edinburgh itself is working in its own right too. The story allows Rankin to explore parts of Scottish history and the sociology of the various religious factions and does it well. The marching bands and the backdrop of the Troubles gives him some great set pieces too. Two worth noting are the scene after Cafferty's bastard son is offed, which gives Rankin the chance to write another two-header, with Rebus and Cafferty in Barlinnie prison. Every word is perfect; from the put down he gives the pathetic prison guard to the glorious line about the calendar. It's a masterclass. Then there's coruscating scene at the march described with brilliance, a rare set-piece from Rankin and provides an early glimpse of the brilliant work he will do in *The Naming of the Dead*.

The truth is that this is very good right up until Mairie Henderson's country and western excursion. Not that this is scene is a problem (no really!), but it's symptomatic, as on paper Mairie Henderson's country and western excursion is a crazy idea and as you read it the reader starts to think, 'hang on this is all a bit crazy' and starts to realise they have been overwhelmed by the huge number of characters and threads.

You could ask, did Rankin goof with the narrative full stop? The plot when related in a summary is reasonably clear: we'll prove it: mysterious Protestant terror organization with links to the police, and North America is exploiting lax police paperwork to steal guns and put them in the hands of Northern Irish terrorist units. The group has a loose cannon to carry out the dirty work of killing people. You see.

Our point is the narrative doesn't help us see this plot clearly enough, Rankin sticking to a first person narrative almost exclusively here. Yet this story really needed to get into the head of Pilmuir villain Davie Soutar, because written as it is, he seems wholly unlikely, and the book is weaker because we don't get this character. We've mentioned the madness of the last set pieces - the riot and the escaping Cafferty but the whole last forty or so pages needed a redraft to make it much more satisfying. As it stands it's a whirlwind of a section and the reader is left reeling and confused and, dare we say, slightly dissatisfied.

Another example is the reveal of the surprising bad guy, let's say, which to be fair, you don't see coming, but you're not **expecting** to see it coming. There's no foreshadowing, so you don't look for the clues, which are all there, although one vital clue is left very tenuous, which Rankin could have helped the reader with. Perhaps Rankin thinks he's writing a gritty police procedural where some of the sleuthing is carried out off-stage, or worked out by Rebus, but Rankin doesn't tell us as much. Rankin may well resent the pleasure some crime fiction readers get from trying to work out the answers, but that's a big chunk of the potential readership feeling a bit let down. He needed to be clearer about what he was trying to do.

The truth is that, as we've noted, the story is four or five characters too heavy and as such without a cleaner narrative the power of the story gets a little lost. For example much as it grates to say it you could lose the whole Cafferty sub-plot and did Mairie Henderson need to be in at all, or is it just to give us a pair of great legs to have described to us? This lack of editorial guidance is a shame because the idea had an awful lot of promise.

Let It Bleed

Published by: Orion 1995

One-line Summary: Our John Rebus arrives at last in a story that weaves in suicides and political favours to the burgeoning hi-tech industries.

Cover: A variety available here: the original cover was a rather stylized painting of a junkie with a large needle under Edinburgh castle, all rendered in purples and reds. Unless you are very lucky to have an original hardback you probably haven't seen it. Somewhere down the line Orion changed their house style and the first paperback edition consists of the future typical atmospheric Edinburgh shots, this time of some steps. Later editions are weirder: one looks like some overgrown weeds by the side of a river.

TV adaptation: Ken Stott's second season's last story! Very, very loosely based on the story, i.e. an ex-con shoots himself and then off we go into a whole new world!

Four things to notice about Let it Bleed:

1) We're into the Rolling Stones era of Rebus, which might surprise latecomers but with it comes the classic Rebus we've been waiting for. It contains Rankin's favourite music quote: "After a drink he likes to listen to the Stones. Women, relationships and colleagues had come and gone but the Stones had always been there. He put the album on and poured himself a final drink. The guitar riff, one of easily half a dozen in Keith's tireless repertoire kicked the album off. 'I don't have much,' Rebus thought, 'but I have this'." It goes without saying, we think that Rankin would have preferred to be a rock star than a writer.

2) Rankin had been putting quotes at the front of his books for a while but as with a lot of things relating to *Let it Bleed* he nails it this time with: 'Without women life is a pub' – Martin Amis , from his novel *Money*. And in this book we get the first real sense of Rebus's relationship with alcohol. It's very influenced by the hard-drinking of Rankin's American heroes, although in later books it's clear Rebus is not alcoholic per se, more a drunk. Here, he clearly *does* have a problem though, and his forty–eight hour bender is one of the saddest images we ever have of Rebus anywhere in the books. Our hero has never seemed so lost and out of control: Rebus is usually in complete control…Rankin claimed it celebrated the Scots' relationship with alcohol, but it also nods to Lawrence Block again, and Matt Scudder.

3) Rankin claims this also has his favourite opening to a Rebus book, with our hero pursuing some kids in a car chase through Edinburgh that ends with a crash, the car hanging precariously off the Forth Road Bridge. Rankin calls this his "Hollywood moment". You'll find out the reasons why below.

4) What is also interesting is how Rebus treats Patience here. His daughter has moved in with her, putting a wedge between Rebus and her, and the way they effectively split up - with Patience bringing him pieces of dead cat - is remarkably macabre. As we'll see later Rankin had concluded that girlfriends get in the way and so Patience, like a lot of previous tropes, is being jettisoned to make room for a whole new set of tropes, which will be much more permanent and iconic.

First and Lasts:

First appearance of Professor Gates, named after the Oxford bar's owners and probably brought in because Rankin realised he hadn't been writing post mortem scenes correctly. In Scotland two pathologists are needed, rather than the one in the USA, or in England. This allows for corroboration of the evidence.

Although Marie Henderson confirmed that Rebus likes the Rolling Stones in *Mortal Causes* here is the first true link to Rebus adoring the band. It's also the first of three books named after Rolling Stones albums (who would do a thing like that!?).

It's the last appearance of Fart Lauderdale, which coincides with the reintroduction of the great Gill Templer as a major character. Last mention of Nell Holmes too. First brief mention DC 'Rat Arse' Reynolds, who will be a more prominent comedy figure towards the end of the series.

First iconic use of The Chair, Rebus's favourite place to sleep, and the first time Rebus uses a 'cellular phone' in the proper novels.

It's also the first time Rankin uses the 'Born in the Kingdom of Fife' statement in his biography and is the first of the true 'three-pronged' story line books.

Background:

Although the title will always be linked to the Rolling Stones it is also a play on a variety of things going on here. So the title is obviously from the great album (the one with the cake on the cover made by Delia Smith) but it also refers to his need to bleed the radiators at the cold flat on Arden St in a cold, Scottish winter. It also vaguely alludes to the poison in his tooth and also the political poison that Rebus just cannot let lie associated with toadying up to the entrepreneurs in Silicon Glen. It's true that this is one of Rankin's more political novels and runs parallel to *Strip Jack*, although the structure really reminds us this is a sequel of sorts to *Hide and Seek,* but done properly, with a much more plausible premise.

Rebus's sudden adoration of the Stones is a little bit hard to take; remember he started as a jazz fan, but as with many things to do with Rankin, it mirrors his own enlightenment to the greatest rock band of them all. As he recites in his introduction to the book, he bought the LP within ten years of writing this book and loved the audio quality, which he appreciated through his job in the hi-fi magazine office.

The opening scene is very un-Rankin in that it has a filmic quality we rarely see. We're not saying Rankin doesn't do action but it's not something we associate with the Rebus stories, so this electrifying car chase on the Forth Road bridge with the swirling snow is quite wonderful. Rankin was driven to writing more action because he was still barely making enough money to survive as a professional writer and felt the only way to make a living was to transfer his writing to the small screen. He wasn't getting very far with that either: ITV cop show *The Bill* was too formulaic and he got fed up with the BBC and their barriers preventing bringing the Rebus show to television: but this might explain the blurb on the back of the American edition of the book (see below).

Rankin was asked to write a final chapter for the American market. As you may notice the book ends leaving us not really knowing if the bad guys get brought to justice. Rankin wasn't impressed by the request but complied (he wasn't famous enough to refuse - yet). The chapter has never appeared in any UK version so it's not well known over here. It's not on the Google books versions either. We picked up an American print and the chapter consists of barely a page, but it does tie up the loose ends, or at least allows us an insight into what happened. Call us dumb but we think the chapter works really well...

What we *really* liked however was the blurb on the back of this book, which we will quote, if we may…the bracketed words are ours: "Edgar-nominated author of the John Rebus novels - which the BBC has optioned (did they?) - and recipient of England's (you mean Britain's) coveted (for the book after this) Gold Dagger award, plus the prestigious Raymond Chandler Fulbright scholarship, Scotland native Ian Rankin stands as one of today's most talented young writers. Now see for yourself why Rankin shines...

In the dark days and biting windstorms of an Edinburgh Winter two drop-out kids dive off the towering Forth Road bridge (well, big anyway). A civic officer is spattered by a grisly gun blast (is it?). Two suicides and a murder don't add up (that's three suicides and no murder), unless Rebus can crunch the numbers (what is he, an accountant?). Following a trail that snakes through stark alleys (well one) and sad bars (fair enough), shredded files and lacerated lives Rebus finds himself up against an airtight murderous conglomerate on the make in every arena of power." Sounds like a different book to us!

Anyway, back to the final chapter, Rankin was still annoyed by this years later and in an interview said this: "The reason the crime novel has not been taken as seriously as it should be by the academics and the literary establishment is because of that sense of closure. There's that sense that things are wrapped up too neatly in a crime novel, therefore it is not like real life. Having talked to cops, sometimes they don't *get* that sense of closure. Sometimes they get the wrong guy for the right reasons or the right guy for the wrong reasons. They're not always satisfied even if they get a result in a case. I wanted to bring some of that feeling across. I wanted the novels to be realistic to the extent that it isn't always wrapped up at the end. Sometimes readers ask me what happened to a certain character or what happened next and I tell them, 'You have to decide what happens. It's finished as far as I'm concerned and you have to decide what happens next.'"

Things That Don't Make Sense:

The old-school Rebus fan will say the Stones conversion, but that's just being naughty, because he hardly mentioned them at the start of the series, although we must note that any true jazz cat would detest the Stones, blues being seen as a very primitive form of music in comparison.

As far as the plot goes there is continuity galore here, like reusing the nurse from *Strip Jack* for no real reason, but conversely there is no real explanation as to how Sammy got to be living with Patience! One or the other Ian.

Something that *does* make sense but might make you think is in the section where Rebus is interviewing Derwood Charters. During their verbal chess game Rankin writes: 'Rebus was learning he must needs be oblique.' Here Rankin is using 'needs' not as a verb but an adverb. It's rather archaic and makes the contemporary reader step out of the story to work out what he's saying. It's perfectly grammatically correct though, just surprising.

The kids' suicide at the start, although dramatic is a little - unlikely from a motivational point of view, and add to this their crashing onto HMS Descant and it becomes hugely unlikely. Also HMS Descant is a made-up name for a ship, which makes no sense if you look at how weird and lengthy the list of names assigned to Her Majesty's naval ships is. It would have been easier to use a real one.

Oh, and dentists aren't Doctors.

Musical References:

Of course the book is named after a song! Brief references to James Taylor and Carly Simon, then the Stones all the way apart from a rather obvious Neil Young nod (*The Needle and the Damage Done*), Dave and Ansel Collins' *Double Barrel* was very popular reggae track in late 1960's and will be mentioned again in the next book, and Jimi Hendrix's *Electric Ladyland* gets a nod as a tape he left at Patience's house.

Review:

Superb. Rankin gives us a cold, bleak tale set in a cold, bleak winter. The plot is easy to follow, coincidence kept to a minimum and Rebus detects and probes beautifully. Rankin in a tweet, (where he was admittedly being funny) claims to have read this fewer than three times. We suspect it's actually one of his favourites. This, more than any other book *does* give us the formula for a classic Rebus tale: dark, dirty Edinburgh, dry wit, and a lot of insight into Rebus's head. He's a detective who sleeps in his armchair, his drinking and smoking out of control. Perhaps there's not enough humour, but if you've been looking for the real start of the Rebus series then this has the best claim. Rebus is at his PI best, not really working as a police officer. The shooting party scene is a glorious example of Rebus outside his comfort zone, however it doesn't quite work. It needed something else, not the red herring we get.

At the same time this is deadly serious, no levity at all, barely a pub scene, barely a smile. A rare use of metaphor with Rebus's tooth letting the poison out summing it up. This is mature, and layered, dripping with allusion and metaphor. Ok, the suicide that kicks this off is a little silly and the ending is unsatisfactory given the build-up but this is a great entry point to the series and it foreshadows the next book, which exploded Rankin to the big time. And it hasn't really aged bar one Natural Law party reference. It's 1995 for sure with that.

Black and Blue

Published by: Orion 1996

One-line summary: Rebus works on a lot of cases including an old serial killer, a copycat serial killer, another old case involving police corruption that only he'd know the answer to and a brutal 'assisted suicide' of an oil worker.

Cover: Without exception all the covers so far have a sort of moody forest on the front. See Firsts and Lasts for more. The first edition had the fluorescent green author heading.

TV adaptation: This was the first to be filmed and starred hot-at-the-time John Hannah. Essentially everyone's a lot sexier and a lot of the subsidiary plots have been removed. An aside, Rankin has the box set, but has never watched the series. He does not want his Rebus to be contaminated by the mannerisms of the lead actor, as happened to Colin Dexter's Morse. In 2013 it was adapted for Radio.

Five things to notice about Black and Blue:

1) This is Rankin's favourite Rebus book and it was of course Rankin's breakthrough novel. It sold four times as many copies as his previous books and won awards. Rankin says that until that point, he had worried that he would never make it as a writer. "Suddenly I thought, I know what I'm doing. I'd written a book that was better and more complex than my previous work."

2) The title, as is well documented, is not only a Stones album, but a reference to the colours associated with oil and police - and the colour of bruises. Rebus does take a lot of punishment in this book. And Rebus is still not really

working as a police officer. He goes off on his own; this time on a recommended holiday, avoiding DCI Ancram's inquiries into an old case where he might be a crucial witness.

3) This won awards, the major one being the UK Crimewriters' Association Golden Dagger for the best novel of 1997. It deserves it, but what is curious is that no other Rankin book ever won again, although *Dead Souls* was nominated. This strikes us as odd, given some of the winners in the 21st Century. I mean was Jose Carlos Samoza's *Athenian Murder* really better than *Resurrection Men* in 2003?

4) At last Rebus's car is explicitly described as being a Saab, but the make (a 900) will elude us for one more book. Rankin clearly has a soft spot for Saabs because he'd already given Gregor Jack and Professor Curt Saabs, and car marques are barely mentioned in this series unless they're posh, or vital evidence. Rankin, in a tweet dated March 2013 said that Rebus's Saab would keep going until no replacement parts/mechanic could be found. (#Rebussaab).

5) Bill Paterson was the voice of the early audiobooks of the Rebus novels but when it came to producing *Black and Blue* Paterson said he was unable to do it. The reason was, according to Rankin, that Paterson's brother had been a suspect in the original Bible John case. Not a serious one, he just happened to vaguely match the description, as did a lot of men at the time. The whole experience proved highly traumatic to Paterson and his family and he did not want to be a part of remembering the experience.

Firsts and lasts:

This is cheating but we get perhaps only our second description of Rebus here via a surprisingly detailed description of Dod Bain, who is described as '5'11", a couple of inches shorter and maybe ten pounds lighter than Rebus.' It's not much but it's all we'll get. This seems to be a good time for us to nail our colours to the mast: we think Rebus resembles Les McKeown, the Bay City Roller's singer. Go on, google him.

We get our first brand name designer: Nike. The first fat word count for the airport bookstores, and the first with the Orion 'moody' covers, which will become a hallmark of the series, but not often relate to the action within. Another hallmark of the mid-period books are music segues and we get our first one here. Talking of music, this is the first book where the Rolling Stones really really start to dominate, with Rankin adding a James Ellroy, he of the tartan noir, quote to the front, and emphasizing one word etc. By now, as we'll see Ellroy was *the* big influence.

This is the only book where Rebus is in exile at Craigmillar station but this reallocation allows this to have a relaunchy feel to it, so if you prefer it's the last relaunch of the range.

First appearance of Jack Morton for a while, reformed from the alcoholic of *Knots and Crosses* and even persuades Rebus to go dry – sort of. This is the last appearance of Brian Holmes, who finally quits to save his marriage. First appearance of another bête noir for Rebus: ACC Colin Carswell.

We get the final *Doctor Who* reference, although it's the same joke as before; the first use of the classic 'wooly suit' put-down for a uniformed officer, and 'biscuit tin' for a cell. This is probably due to his reading matter (see below). It's also the last time Rankin attempts a sex scene, thank goodness.

Rankin is back to mentioning slum estates by name: Pilton named here, not Pilmuir. Also, the last mention homeless guy from the short story in *A Good Hanging.*

This is the last book written entirely in France. Oh and this is the last title that's x and x, almost by mistake.

Background:

To quote Rankin: "I remember delivering *Black and Blue*. I'd written about four other novels (sic) by then, and my publishers were getting ready to chuck me because I was midlist. I was ticking over. I was selling enough copies to go into profit but just barely, and they were running out of options. They'd toured me, they'd done promotional tea towels and mugs, they'd tried to get the booksellers onside, and they'd spent some money on advertising, but the books kept selling a few thousand and a few thousand and a few thousand. (But) I knew *Black and Blue* was a much better book than previous books, a much more complex book and a much more successful book. What happened to trigger that transition? Oh, I think lots of things happened. The books before that had been my apprenticeship, and I suddenly realized you could do a lot more than I'd been doing. You could make it quite convoluted. You could take your character out of his comfort zone – take him out of Edinburgh altogether. The book could be darker. I could introduce real elements like a real life serial killer, Bible John, who was never caught. I'd learnt a lot from James Ellroy about using real characters and real crimes in your books, and putting in some historical perspective. So I had Rebus going into libraries and reading newspapers from the '60s, getting a sense of how Scotland had changed from the '60s to what was then the late '80s and early '90s." – The Crime Interviews, Len Wanner.

As the quote above suggests this is the book that moved Rankin into the big league. It all came together perfectly. Rankin says the opening murder idea came from a friend of his called Lorna whose brother was an oil industry worker and had exactly the same incident happen to him with the bag on the head and the tools. To her *that* was the story: to Rankin it was the start. Once he had the oil industry the story wrote itself. But there's more than that. As Rankin himself notes he had served an apprenticeship and he had lots of ideas and they spewed out on the page. He was also angry; angry at the fate of his son Kit. Kit is Rankin's younger son and suffers from a genetic disorder called Angelman syndrome which means that, though big for his age, he cannot walk or talk. Their house in France was tumbledown, Kit needed specialist help and money was a problem. Rankin fought off his panic attacks (remember he gave them to Rebus in *Strip Jack*) by driving fast and screaming along the lanes. Getting to the bottom of Kit's medical problems and his frustrations with his inability to understand French well enough to hear what the doctors said made him angry. He wanted to be God rather than let God run his life and Rebus took the brunt... It all went in to this book. There is an irony, Rankin says, in the fact that Kit made him a better writer.

Black and Blue is particularly vivid is because of its description of the oil boom and its transforming impact on so much of Scottish - and, indirectly, British - life. However you get the feeling that when Rebus says he doesn't know much about the oil industry he's vocalising Rankin's guilt at his own and perhaps the Scottish people's ignorance and ambivalence at the industry. He clearly researched the industry well, using the publicity blurb oil companies love to give out and it's clearly on the page. And although Rankin didn't get to visit Shetland he does a good job of describing it. This is still true reading it today in an era where Anne Cleeves' wonderful Shetland-based detective series starring Jimmy Perez makes the islands much more familiar.

It goes without saying that James Ellroy was *the* big influence on this book. Look at how he is mentioned in the quote at the start, but look at the quote below from Rankin about how he knew *Black and Blue* was going to be big.

"I felt it. When I started plotting it and started writing it, I could feel that it was a different kind of book. It was initially given an injection from my close and passionate reading of James Ellroy. I went on a real tear with him. If you read the opening pages of *Black and Blue*, there's a real James Ellroy feel to them - very staccato sentences with a lot of slang that you might not know but that gives a lot of mood and character. I knew the book was going to be a lot darker and use a real-life case, which I had never done before."

So Ellroy gave him the big landscapes which Rankin wanted to explore but there were other sources too. *Black and Blue* was so important that it merited its own academic discussion. Gill Plain wrote a critical reader on *Black and Blue* for Continuum classics in 2000. It's worth reading and also cites Anthony Powell's lengthy A *Dance to the Music of Time* novels as a source, saying Rankin became seduced by the decades of layers that are structured into the books. If you also mentions Irvine Welch at this point whose *Trainspotting* was super hip and used the argot Rankin started to use.

There are some lovely in-jokes in the book too. The Dancing Pigs is the most well-known. This was the name of a band that Rankin was in aged 19, transferred to a famous rock group in the fictional world. Rankin felt it was cooler to use that than an established band like U2, and he was right, though of course with *that* name they would get nowhere in Muslim countries. Also, fellow Scottish writer Iain Banks gets a mention via his book *Whit*, his most recent at the time of writing. Iain Banks and Irvine Welch were the top Scottish writers at the time, and Rankin was about to join them. Other in-jokes include the false names he gave Stanley Toal and Eve when they go to confess at the station: Madeleine Smith and William Pritchard. These names just happened to be on a page of a random book in front of Rebus in the Bible John incident room. Both were murderers named in the book *The Square Mile of Murder* by Jack House in 1961, book related to horrific Glasgow murders. Finally, Moose Maloney, a random hood Rebus adds to an interview, must be a nod to the baddie Moose Malloy in Marlowe's *Farewell my Lovely*.

Ironically the reason why this book is so popular and so resonant is the inclusion of the real-life Bible John in the narrative, returning to take revenge on the upstart Johnny Bible. Indeed, the TV dramatization ignores the oil industry section entirely and focusses on just that. Even at the time Rankin must have known that basing a story Bible John and then getting Bible John to narrate parts was risky, and in the afterword of the original book he noted his fear when a TV documentary suggested another name for Bible John. Modern thoughts suggest that Bible John was actually convicted killer Peter Tobin. He was jailed aged 60 for a similar crime and no doubt he was active a lot earlier. The photo fit of the young Tobin looks very similar. So was it a mistake to include him? Yes and no; yes because it's probably not really right to fictionalize such a brute, but no because the use of Bible John really put this book out there. For example this was the second Rebus book we read, having been mildly unimpressed by *The Hanging Garden*. This sealed the deal for many readers, including us.

Things That Don't Make Sense:

The first edition manages to spell lasso wrong. Oops; in fact talking about the practicalities of bookmaking, Rankin admits that the publishers went all out on the cover here, putting his name in a new bright green font and putting a 'spooky' forest on the cover. Yet there isn't a forest in the story anywhere. It's spook for the sake of spook, which reminds us of the reissue of *Mortal Causes* that had that turret on it for no reason. Do cover artists ever read books? An aside, but around this time a young writer called Joanne Rowling was about to get her first book published. If you can find an early printing of *Harry Potter and the Philosopher's Stone* then pause to laugh at the depiction of the 'ancient' wizard Professor Dumbledore on the back cover as young redheaded man. It was corrected at around the 20th reprint!

Still on the book itself the blurb on the back says Rebus is working on four cases at once, but it's six. Technically - Bible John, Johnny Bible, the Lenny Spaven enquiry, Gill Templer's big case -

74

which segues into all the others, Alan Mitchison, Brian Holmes' problem. And are people supposed to remember Jim Stevens from *Knots and Crosses*? And while we're there would the *Knots and Crosses* case really have been called the 'knots and crosses' case?

"I can see clearly now" was recorded by Johnny Nash, not Marvin Gaye.

When Rebus is knocked unconscious outside his hotel he does very well to have a clear memory of what happened. It would be more typical to have complete memory loss of everything prior to the kicking. As this happens all the time in fiction we'll let it go.

We're going to say it: Bible John as a narrator *was* a mistake. Irrespective of whether Bible John is Peter Tobin, or any number of theories it's probably in poor taste to fictionalise a monster who is possibly still alive. Adding Bible John to the mix here gives it a ghoulish edge, but there's no need, there's plenty going on anyway. Perhaps a coda at the end where Rebus realises he met Bible John in that bar would have been better? Contemporary reviews thought so too. "Adding Bible John was a brilliant device but Rankin fails to capitulate on this brilliant gambit" – Marcel Berlins in the Times. Looking back in 2015 this still rings true. In an age of instant access to Wikipedia a reader can now see that Bible John here isn't Bible John.

There is a bit of a problem with the timings when it comes to the protest ship at the oil rig in the North Sea. If it takes Rebus in a helicopter three hours to get there and let's assume a chopper goes at 140 knots, we're looking at the oil rig being say 300 nautical miles away from Aberdeen, which is about right. Well the protest ship boat as described in text would probably at best do 15 knots. So it would have taken at the most optimistic 20 hours to get to the rig, probably longer. For Braid Hair to have got to the rig at the same time as Rebus she would have had to have set off BEFORE she had been even seen by Rebus at the conference the day before!

Musical References:

Blimey, this is where music gets really important, so we'll skip past the book title, the inevitable Stones references and the 'I can see clearly now' error and get to the rest:

Segues:

It's A Sin - Pet Shop Boys, So What? - Miles Davis. Fool To Cry - Rolling Stone.
Don't Look Back - Bob Dylan. Framed - Alex Harvey Living In The Past - Jethro Tull
Alright Now – Free - Been Down So Long - The Doors
God Only Knows - Beach Boys More Trouble Every Day - Frank Zappa & The Mothers of Invention

Chapter Title:

'Ave The Leopards - The Bathers

Songs played in the flat:

Meddle (LP) - Pink Floyd

Tubular Bells (LP) - Mike Oldfield

Songs played in the car:

Rock Bottom - Robert Wyatt

Into The Fire - Deep Purple

Songs hummed in the shower:

76

Puppy Love - Donny Osmond
What Made Milwaukee Famous - Rod Stewart

Heard on a phone line:

In A Broken Dream - Python Lee Jackson
John, I'm Only Dancing - David Bowie
Mouldy Old Dough - Lieutenant Pigeon

Sundry other references:

Dead End Street - The Kinks – his life was turning into
Albatross - Fleetwood Mac – slow song at a nightclub
Double Barrel - Dave and Ansel Collins
Zero The Hero – Gong
Hi Ho Silver Lining - Jeff Beck

Review:

As *The Independent* wrote in 1997: "Rankin certainly merits his
Gold Dagger for the sheer cunning of his intrigue and the morose,
but oddly moving, realism of his hero's dysfunctional existence.
Rankin depicts the Wild North with relish that has precious few
rivals in the "literary" novel. How many (Will) Selfs or (Ian)
McEwans could take us into the raucous frontier-town dives of
Aberdeen, through the vast Shetland terminal at Sullom Voe, or onto
the platforms planted in the icy waves? Yet North Sea oil is one the
great, hidden themes of modern British culture: an invisible Gulf
Stream that made the climate that bit warmer than it should have
been, but won't endure much longer. It needs its chroniclers in
fiction as well as fact. As ever, good crime writing can reach those
social parts that more genteel operators dare not investigate."

And it *is* one of the great pieces of 90's crime writing. Rebus taken away from his usual haunts is magnificent on every page. Rebus in purgatory at Craigmillar, shit hitting the fan, this feels like a yet another relaunch and my God it works as one, as the reader's interest is immediately piqued. Later, the scenes with Ancram and Rebus in the interview crackle. It's one of our favourite ever scenes where Ancram tries to interrogate Rebus about Lenny Spaven, but Rebus knows all the tricks of the trade. The Aberdeen scenes are uniformly brilliant too and the whole oil terminal setting allows you to learn as well as be engrossed. Rebus is the wounded and seedy cop chasing anything that moves and all the pieces come together in Aberdeen so Rankin can write about the coming of oil. At the time it was so successful it made people read the rest of the books and become Rebus fans.

In terms of writing it's a fine work but there are so many interlinked strands here that you almost wish he'd saved a few for other tales. So much is left at the wayside as the narrative rolls on towards its conclusion. You have the Lennie Spaven case which looks like a nice cold case story on its own. You have Johnny Bible who is sort of tied in but is made a peripheral to a drugs case. The drugs case itself has a genuine psychopath at the helm, who barely gets two pages. You have the wonderfully evil Toal family, who we'll never see again. And of course we have the history lesson of Bible John. That's a lot, and come on readers, does anybody remember why Alan Mitchison was actually killed? Thought not.

Having said that complaining about it being almost too crammed is pointless because that is what makes the Rebus books what they are. Our beloved Rebus is a mess and he will be operating like this from now on and we wouldn't have it any other way. Rankin isn't and never has really been interested in the whodunit aspect of his work, more what is it like to live in this society where such things are possible? So we restate the point again. Rankin is a crime writer he uses crime to open up the core of the society he really wants to write about and the deserved success of this brilliant book allowed him to fully pursue this theme. This was the bridge between the cod writer earning a living and the award winning social commentator.

The Hanging Garden

Published by: Orion 1998

One-line Summary: Rebus has an almost personal vendetta against Tommy Telford, new gangster on the block, whose tendrils spread out to other organised crime around the world. Also, Rebus is looking into the past of an old Nazi war criminal.

Cover: A twisty road in a forest at night. Anyone... Later editions have a hand pressed against glass, and for the most recent we're back to forests. Again, anyone?

TV adaptation: The second episode of the John Hannah incarnation.

Six things to notice about The Hanging Garden:

1) As we saw in *Black and Blue* Rankin is in full James Ellroy mode by this stage. He's acknowledged writers before of course but few have had such an effect on his style. For those who don't know James Ellroy his style is staccato and brutal, all inessential words removed and Rankin does it here as well. Ellroy (probably joking) claims his style is simply like that because he always goes over the required page length and cuts the words down by removing inessential words from sentences. For example from *LA Confidential*: "shrieks from the courtyard; running feet on gravel. Meeks dropped the shotgun, stumbled to the wall. Over to the men, tasting blood - point blank head shots." You can find similar writing in the first part of *The Hanging Garden*, and at the start of *Black and Blue*. If you don't like staccato Rankin, well relax because he gets over

his Ellroy obsession by the next book, from here on in Rankin's main influence is…himself

3) Long-term readers can start to play the 'spot the change in rank' game. The Farmer is back as a DCS and Ormiston is definitely a DC here, after changing rank twice in *Mortal Causes*. In *Dead Souls* and *Set in Darkness* Siobhan will briefly be a DS before her actual promotion in *Resurrection Men*. Even weirder Bill Pryde isn't given a rank anywhere in this book, as if it's just too complicated to even write down. We'll be monitoring this don't you worry.

4) The title comes from a Cure song released as a single in 1982. It's from the album *Pornography*. Whether Rankin is a big Cure fan, or just liked the idea of the title because of events in the book isn't clear but various excerpts from the lyrics are used throughout to introduce the book sections. Rankin tells a nice story about obtaining permission to use the lyrics which we'll come to later. For the Cure fans out there are other references in the book, although Rebus (clearly not a Cure fan) doesn't recognise the name of the amusement arcade 'Fascination Street' as another Cure single. And the song *Mr. Pink Eyes* is used to great effect, if a little forced.

5) Readers may have picked up our cynicism about Rebus as an actual alcoholic and this is an interesting place to pick up on it. Again Matt Scudder, the alcoholic PI is a big influence, but Rebus *isn't* an alcoholic in most of the books. Whether anyone likes it or not Rebus isn't AA material either. He drinks but he enjoys it, it doesn't control him in most books. It's more a habit than an illness. After the events in *Black and Blue* Jack Morton prompted Rebus to eschew alcohol and in this book he is essentially on the wagon. Now this is a brilliant twist to the Rebus stereotype, but is pretty much ruined by whoever's decision it was to structure the novel the way it is, where Rebus downs a

quarter bottle of whisky very early on in the narrative before we know there's a 'dry' theme: so it's an opportunity wasted rather than a masterstroke.

6) Rankin doesn't personify his muse in the way for example Nick Cave does, but he is always surprised by how it works. *The Hanging Garden* is a good case in point. As we will see Rankin often writes a rough first draft and never knows who did it until the end. In *The Hanging Garden* he claims he didn't know who did it until the second draft! As Rankin notes, he does the detective work as well during the first draft and usually the murderer pops out as he writes. His muse simply guides him…

First and Lasts:

First appearance of Bill Pryde, he of the lack of rank. He's a nice, cautious plodder to counter the more wildcard Rebus. Also, welcome DI Bobby Hogan from Leith CID, who's a decent bloke for Rebus to buddy up with. At the same time we get last appearances and mentions of London boys DI Abernethy and DI Flight, and it's the last appearance of Jack Morton too, sadly.

Although we have had mobile phones in the series before, this is the first book where Rebus definitely owns one. He doesn't seem bothered by it either, suggesting common usage. It's interesting that we never see Rebus using the notoriously bad police communication devices known as Airwave, which is halfway between a mobile and a walkie talkie.

First brief mention of the Morvena casino, a fictionalized place that Rebus DEFINIFTELY GOES IN to watch Matsumoto, see *Death is Not the End*. And it could be the last time Rebus listens to jazz, as he's playing an Eddie Harris album in his flat at one point, and there's some on the radio.

Oh, and this is the last book Rankin worked on in France.

82

Background:

Rankin tells a nice story about Robert Smith, lead singer of the Cure giving permission to use the lyrics by simply asking for a few signed copies of the book, although the part where Rankin claimed to not have a clue where to send the signed copies rings a bit false, Surely he just contacts the people he contacted to get the original permission!

As we've noted this was the last book Rankin conceived in France before returning to Scotland. There were lots of reasons for this but one was to get more convenient and useful medical treatment for Kit. Rankin and family moved into a three-bedroom flat in the city but couldn't really afford the mortgage on the writing income alone. He was about to have a big hit by his standards (*Black and Blue*) and critical acclaim wasn't far away. Before he left the Dordogne for good he made one last trip to a place called Oradour-sur-Glâne, a ruined town left exactly as it was after a Nazi atrocity on 11th June 1944.

In response to an alleged kidnapping of an SS officer 642 villagers were shot or burned by the 4th SS Panzer Grenadier Regiment (Der Führer), not the 3rd SS as Rankin says in his introduction. The instruction had been to take 30 hostages and make them talk, but it quickly got out of hand and led to one of the worst atrocities in the war. The village has been left exactly as it was and Rankin was very moved by what he saw. He writes in the reprint introduction to The *Hanging Garden* that he was also outraged that 'The General' who gave the order was freed by the allies and lived free in Germany until the end of his days. As ever Rankin tells a good story but this statement needs clarification. The man who gave the order wasn't 'the General' but SS Brigadefuhrer Sylvester Stadler, who instructed Sturmbannfuhrer Adolf Dietmann to round up 30 men, but not massacre 642 people. Stadler court-martialed Dietmann, but Dietmann died in battle soon after, some reports suggesting he committed 'suicide by soldier' by getting deliberately shot, so traumatized by how the massacre ended up going. 'The General' was Heinz Lammerding who did indeed live out his days in Germany but *was* actually sentenced to death at the related trial in 1953. West Germany refused to extradite him, according to other sources. Either way it's a powerful story, and should be better known. Some sources suspect that as it happened around the same time as D-Day it was overlooked in the euphoria. Whatever the facts Rankin wanted to write about it. As he himself noted:

"It had a powerful effect on me, that place. I wanted to write about it, but couldn't figure out how. Finally I thought, I'll write about a suspected war criminal living in Edinburgh, quietly, and Rebus has to work out whether it's worth prosecuting him after 50 years. So I went back to Edinburgh, having written half the story, only to find that there was a suspected Nazi war criminal living quietly in Edinburgh. And a TV documentary crew had made a film about him and he'd sued them and taken them to court. And this was all going on while I'm sitting on this book I thought was a novel." This meant that Rankin had to make sure his Nazi had no resemblance to the living alleged Nazi.

This book is also famous for what happens to Sammy. Rankin said this when asked about writing about his son's disability. 'It's possible. I almost did it in the Rebus novels when I put his daughter in a wheelchair, after Kit was diagnosed. I decided if my son wasn't going to walk, his daughter wasn't going to walk, so she was hit by a car. But then I thought, "What a spiteful thing to do", so she made a full recovery.

The Cafferty/Rebus bond is now firmly in place and Rebus selling his soul to the devil is beautifully seductive. It mirrors the way Cafferty will help Siobhan in *The Naming of the Dead.*

Things That Don't Make Sense:

Is a straight fuck *really* cheaper than a blow job? We're no experts of course, but really?

Patience has clearly forgiven Rebus for cat slaughter but doesn't quite know what hunky dory means. Neither makes much sense to us!

The big problems here concern the East European characters. Let's start with Candice: her lack of English is problematic straight away. Firstly, of all the ex-communist countries the former Yugoslavia *did* teach English in schools and most young people had a working knowledge of English. An aside, we were living in Berlin in 1994 learning German and a Bosnian boy Candice's age was in the class too. He spoke little German but his English was fine. So Candice's would more than likely speak English well, and even if she didn't she wouldn't pick it up *that* quickly! This is despite the fact that Candice seems a bit thick; she doesn't even know what a golf course looks like! Finally would she know western letters? The Serbs used the Cyrillic alphabet. In addition, while we're tearing Rankin apart the whole name thing is dodgy. Candice isn't a very Yugoslav name, becoming popular mainly in the USA in the 1970s because of Candace Bergen. And no you can't say Candace's dad was a fan, in Yugoslavia names had to be on the official list, usually saints names. It's possible Candice is just a prostitute name but there's no reference to this.

Now let's move to Tarawicz. No one seems to know if Tarawicz is from Chechnya or Serbia, yet his surname sounds Polish to us, the 'wicz' means male offspring: well, it would if it was spelt correctly - as Tarowicz. Taradzic would have been more likely Slavic spelling, like with Radnan Karadzic. Ironically Cafferty gets it right and is corrected by Rebus. Finally, Tarawicz's use of the phrase 'I'm struck to the quick' is incongruous to say the least.

Elsewhere, we have the usual 'he's writing a private eye plot' problems of a DI travelling to Newcastle for no reason, when all they would do is pick up the phone.

It's unlikely Telford could have got the neighborhood so well sewn up in such a short time; we say this because he simply hasn't been mentioned before this book, so whole swathes of pensioners and businesses needed to become part of his empire very quickly.

Rebus quotes the often said urban myth that Pink Floyd's *Wish you were Here* album smelt of burning flesh when you removed the plastic seal. It didn't.

The whole AIDS storyline is included in this section too. Not the plausibility, just the inclusion, which is clearly just to crank up the tension. Worse is that it's unresolved at the end and never mentioned again. We accept that Rankin sees loose ends as a hallmark of the Rebus books, using the whole 'life is a series of loose ends' argument, but to forget about it completely seems just daft.

Nearly there, Rankin half gives away the plot of *Knots and Crosses* a rare slip. Oh, and Siobhan is a DS on p 308.

Musical references:

Deep Breath…
Let's assume you have noticed the Cure references.

Using songs to add piquancy to a scene:

Although Rankin started doing this a lot in *Black and Blue* it becomes epidemic here. For example on speaking to his ex-wife on the phone re Sammy, "he tried to find some feeling for her. Richard and Linda Thompson 'withered and died.'"

Others:

Paint It Black - The Rolling Stones – a reference to Pretty Boy
Kid Charlemagne - Steely Dan
Lonely Little Girl - Frank Zappa & The Mothers Of Invention
Wishful Sinful - The Doors
Out Of Time - Chris Farlowe
Cruising For Burgers - Frank Zappa & The Mothers Of Invention
Family Snapshot - Peter Gabriel
Chocolate Girl - Deacon Blue
New Kid In Town - The Eagles
Accidents Will Happen - Elvis Costello
Just Wanna See His Face - The Rolling Stones
Still... You Turn Me On - Emerson Lake and Palmer
Paper Plane - Status Quo
Goin' Home - Ten Years After
There Is A Way - Leonard Cohen
Soul Survivor - The Rolling Stones
Can You See The Real Me - The Who
Double Crossing Time - John Mayall's Bluesbreakers

Hi-fi songs

Hardnose The Highway - Van Morrison
Wish You Were Here - Pink Floyd
Argus - Wishbone Ash
Rock n' Roll Circus - The Rolling Stones – though he only plays the
Stones tracks – it's compilation – sort of
Astral Weeks - Van Morrison
Aladdin Sane - David Bowie
Quadrophenia - The Who
Unknown LP - Eddie Harris

Jokes
Tower Of Babel - Elton John
Faint-heart And The Sermon - Peter Hammill
Hunky Dory - David Bowie

Cassettes in a stolen car

Marriage of Figaro
Verdi's Macbeth
Greatest Hits - Roy Orbison

Car songs
Psycho Killer - Talking Heads
(jazz on radio) - Astrid Gilberto, Stan Getz, Art Pepper, Duke
Ellington

Sundry mentions
Emerson Lake and Palmer
The Enid
Yes (triple album, presumably "Yessongs")

Crazy - Patsy Cline
Someone Saved My Life Tonight - Elton John
Iron Maiden – as in the T-shirt Rebus is forced to wear after being
covered in blood – although it's not clear at first read.

Segue (Only one!)

Simple Twist Of Fate - Bob Dylan - Is This What You Wanted -
Leonard Cohen

Oh, and Oasis get three mentions, well they were at their peak

Review:

This is the third time we've read this book and we never want read it again. There is an unremitting bleakness on show here, with few sympathetic characters. It starts off with another intense prologue (the third in a row), which is very James Ellroy but this never lets up. You'll be told *Black and Blue* is the dark one but really it's this. This is the least Rebusy book so far and Rebus barely sets foot in a police station.

There are two major problems with this: Rankin's Ellroy obsession causes the book to have a driving without brakes, relentless, no breath pace, which doesn't fit in with the rest of the series thus far. There's very little of the Edinburgh vignettes which usually characterize his work. This brings us to the second problem: this gangland wall-pissing tale could have been set in any town anywhere in the world. This isn't Rebusy enough and could have starred any number of grizzled cops from around the world in any city in the world.

This is made worse by what we assume is an editorial decision to put Sammy's accident at the start to give the story to give it more emotional punch. Although that is certainly the case it also skews the book into a violent head rush and setting a tone which overwhelms. The truth is the latter part of the book is lot softer and actually rather good, but you've been so exhausted by the first bit you fail to notice.

This leads us to the drinking or the lack of it in this book; because they've put the crash at the start we get Rebus downing whisky in the prologue. This is nothing new or surprising. They have missed the trick that Rebus downing whisky halfway through the book after really trying the teetotal thing is interesting. One has to ask has Rankin realised he now has fans who care about Rebus?

Having said that the plot that Rebus unravels here is quite brilliant and perhaps the most satisfactory we've had from Rankin. Perhaps there are the usual too many coincidences, but the gang warfare tale is lovely despite the impossibility of Telford setting it all up so fast. The ending too is hugely satisfying and by Rankin's standards clear, which allows this book to stand with the other great books, however it is no surprise that the style of this book is never repeated.

Death is not the End

Published by: Orion (1998) - novella

Cover: A sort of moody shot of people dancing in a night club. Shock horror, it sort of fits!

One thing to notice about Death is Not the End:
It's the sub-plot of *Dead Souls* and so causes all sorts of continuity problems with our Rebus timeline. We'll address these in more detail in *Dead Souls.*

Firsts and Lasts:
Very few given the brevity, but it is the first time Rankin published a novella and the first time he directly copied himself, or if you prefer the first time we see Rebus in an alternative universe.

Background:

Firstly it's named after the Bob Dylan song but we always liked to think Rankin was reminded of it by Nick Cave's stunning version on his *Murder Ballads* album released in late 1996. This was written around this time, given the casino error outlined below. We were delighted when Rankin admitted the Nick Cave source in the introduction to *Dead Souls* that accompanied the 2005 reprints.

This was written at the behest of his American publisher, who as we've seen before seemed to be having trouble marketing Rankin in the states. The extra chapter in *Let it Bleed* springs to mind. Once completed the publisher didn't do much with it, so Rankin reworked it into his next book, which must give continuity freaks like us headaches. Ironically when Rankin got more popular in the States this was reissued and it was assumed (judging by reviews on various reader web pages) as some cunning reworking. Sigh…

Given that this was written after *Black and Blue* a missing person theme is unsurprising. Rankin had become interested in missing persons since he'd been researching Bible John and it seemed natural to pursue it. He had also had a conversation with American author and publisher Otto Penzler about vanishing and this too seeped into his thoughts.

The only other thing of note is that Rebus is watching football 'again': apart from his *Strip Jack* aberration he's never shown much interest. This can be argued away by the football subplot here we think.

Things That Don't Make Sense:

Rebus says he's never been in the Morvena casino before, yet he was in it in *The Hanging Garden*. This is probably due to when this was written, see the background section. In fact if we are going chronological none of this makes sense. In *The Hanging Garden* he goes back to Fife and knows a lot more about where the family pictures are. Here he seems to not to have been to Fife recently doesn't know where the photo albums are. He also makes no reference to Sammy's accident .

Verdict:

An anomaly, although faultless in presentation this is a rather lifeless tale which doesn't amount to much and leaves the usual loose ends around. Who was the glam woman? Why did Mee just leave like that? Add to the much better treatment given in *Dead Souls* and so avoiding the continuity problems we can leave this to be quietly forgotten

And the blonde gets a better story in *Dead Souls*.

Dead Souls

Published by: Orion (1999)

One-line Summary: A serial killer returns to Edinburgh and other cases all dance around each other.

Cover: The original hardback had some atmospheric mountains, which sort of fits in with the section involving Carey Oakes' hike. The paperback edition went for misty, atmospheric Edinburgh streets with setts, which is amusing because that part of Edinburgh is hardly seen in this book. Only the 2008 paperback cover with the railings on it could be said to be relevant to the plot.

TV adaptation: The third episode of Series 2, starring John Hannah. It changes a variety of things, including the relationship Rebus has with Janice Mee, who becomes a near recurring character.

Four things to notice about Dead Souls:

1) Of course the obvious thing is that huge chunks of the missing person storyline had previously appeared in the novella *Death is not the End* the year before. Although, as outlined in the previous chapter that had a limited audience, but it does beg the question about how canon are Rebus's adventures? We saw that in *Mortal Causes* Rankin stresses that the events in that book were a fictional take on reality, but in The future we have *The Naming of the Dead, which* is clearly set in 'our' world. How *can* Rebus have two almost identical adventures?

2) As the Rebus books are as much a note of the changing times in Edinburgh and Scotland we should point out the first use of the now ubiquitous American terms for coffee

with Rebus ordering a caffe latte, although he thinks it should still be called a milky coffee.

3) If you don't count the suicide on page 1 then the first body doesn't arrive until p248: a new record.

4) Does Rankin write himself into the book with the reference to 'the writer' in the back room of the Oxford bar, who gives Rebus ideas for books to read? Rankin also makes one cameo appearance in the TV version of *Mortal Causes*, but we probably mentioned that back in that book, didn't we? Oops.

Firsts and lasts:

First book conceived and written in Edinburgh and boy, was Rankin worried about *that*. He was worried that real Edinburgh might stifle the imaginary Edinburgh in his head. He needn't have worried. This became his first proper 'best-seller' on first release.

Although the title of the book is ambiguous and could refer to a song (like the previous four-ish books), it's more likely named after a book, which makes it a first. See below for more on the source.

First appearances of DC Grant Hood and lazy DS George Silvers, which gives us the first good nickname for a while with 'hi ho'; also, the first appearance by DC Phyllida Hawes. Last appearance by the old hack Jim Stevens and it's rather fitting, although one suspects Rankin brought him back because he likes/fancies Mairie Henderson too much to have her receive the fate in store for Stevens in this story.

What else? Last in-reference to high end hi-fi gear as Rebus listens to Jim Stevens's tape on Sennheiser headphones: like they'd be police issue.

In the real world it's the first time Rankin allowed real people to bid at a charity auction for their names to appear in a book. In later years he will allow up to six characters to be named, and fun can be had trying to work out who they are. Here it is only the delightfully named Fern Bogot, whose name, according to Rankin's introduction sounded so false it had to become a prostitute's pseudonym in this book.

It's the first time we note that Rebus adopts his classic 'lean against the wall' when in the interview room technique. Rebus likes it because he's always in the eye line of the person being questioned.

Last mention of Mrs. Cochrane, last appearance of Ox regular Salty Dougary, but he does get a mention in the next book. Last time we see Patience and the final use of the mis-used noun 'trellis table', but at least Rankin knows it's wrong by now.

Oh and it's the last time Rankin uses a music segue in any meaningful sense. We know Rankin reads reviews and has quoted a pointed aside in a *Private Eye* review - 'something like, "His books are just an excuse to tell us what's in his record collection"' – which hurt, so the music starts to get played down a bit after this.

Background:

It could be named after the Joy Division song (like you've heard it) but given the evidence it was more likely inspired by the unfinished book by Nikolai Gogol of the same name from the mid-nineteenth century. The two books within this book are prefaced by quotes from Gogol. The second book's quotation are the last recorded words by Gogol.

As we know the missing person story from *Death is not the End* is reused here but it's more than that. Much of the detail is repeated word for word, or if you prefer – cut and pasted - even if it's in a different order. There are some minor changes admittedly. The geek cop in *Death* is replaced by Phyllida Hawes; the club is moved to Edinburgh and the nature of the mystery blonde is somewhat different. In fact various parts are weaved in as far as p312, before veering off towards the end.

Of course Rankin needed to add more for a full-length novel though, and this may be a good time to look at how Rankin goes about writing his books. In general he writes from January to May, proofing and redrafts are done in June and July. August is for holidays, the book is out in September and he goes on publicity tours in October and November. In late November out comes the green folder. The folder contains newspaper cuttings and scribbled notes on napkins that are ideas and seeds that Rankin has had in the past. Every time an interesting idea occurs to him it goes in the folder and he forgets about it. He only looks at the contents again when he's looking for ideas for the next book.

When it's time to write all these jottings go through a sifting process. As he sifts some ideas go on to become short stories and some become strands for his next book. Nothing gets thrown away, and some things can stay in the folder for ages. This is beautifully illustrated in the BBC documentary *Imagine...Ian Rankin and the Case of the Disappearing Detective,* where a rather tired-looking Rankin plays out the process for the cameras. It would have been how the paedophile idea came to light, and similarly the mis-per case seen in *The Falls* later on. We'll look at this process in more detail when we look at *Standing in Another Man's Grave,* as this was the book the documentary was made to promote.

Back in 'December 1998' his eye was caught by a newspaper article about a mob of 35 people who stood outside the accommodation where a paedophile was residing. (The story is briefly mentioned in the Independent 24th Feb 1997). The Government had recently decided to produce a list of known offenders and where they lived. Newspapers 'acting in the public interest' published some names, causing vigilante groups to appear. None of this is funny but the perhaps apocryphal story of paediatricians being targeted in ignorance drew a smile. This was woven into the mis-pers plot and Rankin used the opportunity to look deeper into such cases. He had already read Andrew O'Hagan's non-fiction book called *The Missing,* which mentioned

96

Bible John, while researching *Black and Blue* and the emotions generated by missing person cases grabbed him strongly. He would continue to cite O'Hagan in later books (*Exit Music* quotes him again). *The Missing* is worth tracking down: part memoir, part investigation, part re-telling of the Fred West victims' stories. It was even adapted into a play in 2009.

The Carey Oakes storyline is more troubling to source but as a serial reader of the bestseller lists Rankin couldn't have failed to have noted how many ex-cons were making money from their stories. The most glaring example at the time Rankin was putting this book together would have been drug king Howard Marks, whose memoir *Mr. Nice* was released in late 1996 and became an international bestseller. The banter and the feeling of sceptisim about the outlandish bits wouldn't have gone unnoticed when creating Carey Oakes.

But, in truth, all this is flannel to cover the real point of this book, which is that Rankin wanted to take Rebus back home to Fife, to Cardenden, where Rankin could interweave his own memories into Rebus's life. Yes, Rankin has always done this but this is the key text. And Rankin's life becomes Rebus's life: the terraced cul-de-sac in Bowhill for Rebus was the same for Rankin (we see it in the documentary), even the school is the same, (but see Things that Don't Make Sense). Janice Mee's reminiscences are Rankin's own family's too. As Rankin himself admits in *Rebus's Scotland*, he writes a lot about Fife because he really wants to understand himself.

The Oxford Bar becomes a rather spiritual place too, with the author even placing himself in the text. As we know Rankin had been drinking there since his university roommate was the barman there and liked it because it was full of ex-cops who could give him stories. But as he drank there he realised it was perfect for Rebus because it had no affectations. An aside: Rankin took Harry, the Ox's barman on a pilgrimage back to his Cardenden local, "and from a position of considerable authority he pronounced it 'the

97

second-worst pub in the world'". Rankin had to agree – "it was 4.30pm and everybody in there wanted to fight. Even the toothless pensioner with the Zimmer frame offered to take us 'outside'."

Things that Don't Make Sense:

The school contradiction here is famous. Rebus states clearly that he went to Auchterderran secondary school: ASS as the badge says, although in *The Black Book* he had gone to school in nearby Cowdenbeath. Rankin is happy to admit the error here, and it's a classic case of Rankin writing his own story rather than Rebus's, as Rankin went to both.

Janice's mum wants to have a 'Bacardi breezes' oops.

As Rebus reminisces in the Ox, Rankin does one of his head hopping perspective shifts, not really seen since *Tooth and Nail*. Rebus remembers the school leavers' dance and Janice punching him unconscious, then, as if tied by the fact that Rebus is unconscious and so he can't narrate, the perspective shifts and Janice narrates. Weird.

When did Siobhan become a DS? She is one on chapter 46 according to Rebus. The promotion actually happens in *Resurrection Men.*

In the alternate universe story *Death is not the End* Rebus has been going to Hibernian games. Here he chides DI Hogan that his (Hogan's) side are going down to the lower division on seeing a copy of a Hibernian fanzine. We know that Rebus almost certainly followed Hearts as a boy and only goes to Hibernian games to hang out with Siobhan but Rankin isn't being helpful.

Finally, we know this is a sacrilegious thing to say but geographically it makes no sense that Rebus's local is the Ox. It's an unlikely local, 1.5 miles from Arden Street - a 30 minute walk, and it's 1.7 miles in the opposite direction from St Leonard's. Given Rebus never mentioned the place before *Mortal Causes* how precisely did it become his local? The answer is of course that the

Ox was *always* a police pub. It's far enough away from cop shops so you wouldn't bump into recently released criminals; which might explain the Ox as a choice superficially but doesn't explain why Rebus is the only cop in there in this fictional world!

Musical references:

Segues:

Sunkissed You're Not – Greenslade If You Feel Like China Breaking - Jefferson Airplane

The Half-Remembered Question - Incredible String Band - Everything Merges With The Night - Brian Eno

Using a song to remind him of something:
Drowned My Life In Fear - Leaf Hound
He Was a Friend Of Mine - The Byrds
We Are Family - Sister Sledge
Tango Whiskeyman – Can
Young and Innocent Days - The Kinks
Buried Alive In The Blues - Janis Joplin

Songs in the flat, or late at night:
Bogeyman - John Entwistle
For Absent Friends – Genesis
Song for Sinking Lovers – Family
The Sound of Love - Tommy Smith
Two Or Three Spectres - Pete Hamill

In the car:
Another Night In The Old City - String Driven Thing

Sundries:
Good Day Sunshine - The Beatles (Carey Oakes sings it)
Le Freak – Chic – Sammy's cassette player
Sailor - Petula

Stones references:

Goats Head Soup (LP) - The Rolling Stones
Stray Cat Blues - The Rolling Stones
Sympathy For The Devil - The Rolling Stones

Karaoke:
My Way, You To Me Are Everything, Baker St, Satisfaction, Space
Oddity, Losing My Religion

Review:

In Rankin's words: "*Dead Souls* I thought I liked, and then I reread
it. No, I don't like this at all and I don't understand what's going on.
Who are these people? What's happening? It was way too
complicated." He then decided he preferred "Some of the early ones,
the wee short ones!"

This is a funny book, not ha ha funny, because it's not one
of the classics but contains some of the best moments from the
Rebus series. The scenes in Cardenden are achingly good, with
Rebus looking at what might have been, and not regretting a
moment his decision to leave: yet the pull of home still getting to
him. Anyone of the same age feels that when they go home and see
old faces who never left. It's like hearing those mid-period Beatles
songs about Liverpool: nostalgic and emotional. Rebus comes more
alive (as is often the case) when he's not playing policeman. This
makes it an important work and one that anchors the Rebus series as
being about things again after the madness of the previous book that

could have been set anywhere. This is about Scotland as much as it is about crime and the pattern is now set.

So is this a great Rebus story? Well, it's written by a man who is starting to earn after his apprenticeship, starting to get a bit of fame and writing with an assured confidence and skill. But although the book's themes are writ large: neglect, lost people, how abuse - both sexual and physical - are passed on, it can sometimes be blurred out by the overwhelming presence of Cary Oakes, who makes this a book about a sick criminal and not the abuse, or the missing person. Sometimes a character just takes a book and runs with it. This is an important work but not the most satisfying for those who like sharp crime stories, as the ending is a typical vague and sad one rather than an all tied up singing and dancing one

We must confess to liking the great fight at the end with, Rebus brilliantly controlling his anger and coming out on top and we get a classic satisfactory/unsatisfactory ending, which Rankin loves - but he's got a bit better at it. The American publishers won't ask him to write an end chapter again.

So this is a book that Rankin doesn't like, but is important to him. The melancholy air and the return to Fife feels cathartic. It has been described as the corporate glue and the novel that brings Edinburgh back into the fold after *Black and Blue* isolated it a bit. It's a must-read for sure, but maybe not first.

Set in Darkness

Published by: Orion (2000)

One line summary: Rebus discovers an old body, Siobhan finds a new body and both get embroiled in a political conspiracy.

Cover: A sort of moody old circular building. Later editions go for shattered glass, or a white-fronted old building, which looks very like Queensberry house – because it is. Both were taken by Ross Gillespie and Tricia Malley (although we're not sure who pressed the button). Rankin had submitted a short story to Edinburgh university alumni magazine (see the short stories at the back) and was impressed by the accompanying picture. He used them for many subsequent covers and, at last, the covers and the plots were starting to mesh.

TV series: None, but it was adapted as a radio series in 2014 starring Ron Donachie.

Five things to notice about Set in Darkness:

1) The title comes from an obscure poem, "The Old Astronomer to his pupil" by Sarah Williams. In the book Rebus's rather unlikely and jammy love interest quotes it in the Ox. Also, Section 1 of the book quotes Deacon Blue - which gives a lovely comment on Scotland, who'd a thought?

2) The book contains two of Rankin's favourite scenes: a pub scene that takes place not in the Oxford Bar, but in the Royal Oak. Rebus decides to nip down to the bathroom, which can be reached without entering the pub. A window looks into the bar and as Rebus glances in, he double takes. There in the bar, singing a Burns song is Cafferty, who

Rebus believes is safely locked up in jail. "Rebus's world is off kilter completely," says Rankin. "I don't always manage to surprise Rebus, but I like the fact that I did this time." He also says his favourite Rebus and Siobhan scene is here too. Sitting together in the car, Rebus (in the driving seat) reaches across Siobhan's legs to retrieve something from the glove compartment. She flinches, thinking he is making a pass at her, and neither of them wants a romantic relationship. "Just that tiny little reaction of her flinching gives a richness to their relationship that a thousand words of trying to spell it out wouldn't do," says Rankin. "A relationship would completely destroy the working dynamic between them."

3) 'Eyes like a frigate's hull' is a phrase that left the estimable former Scottish MP Donald Dewar bemused, but clearly pleases Rankin. We acknowledge it too, it's glorious, although we're sure it leaves the international market cold. 'Eau de bachelor' is another corker, relating to how Rebus' flat smells these days.

4) One of the many clichés you'll read about Rebus is that he has only voted three times and implies his ambivalent attitude. The brilliant passage about the 1979 devolution vote here puts paid to that. Rebus is political but he's also a stubborn old sod and damaged by his past behaviours.

5) It's interesting to see the Rosslyn chapel in Roslin depicted here before Dan Brown got his hands on it two years later in *The Da Vinci Code* (don't make us write a Dan Brown book – the Things That Make no Sense sections would be enormous). Now everyone knows about the place. Here Rankin creates a character called Sithing who ploughs out the usual Templar nonsense. Despite what Sithing and Brown say apparently the chapel looks nothing like the Solomon temple, and there's even some debate about when the chapel was built!

First and Lasts:

As noted, the title is from a poem, which is a first, but it's also another punny title, as Rankin argues that the long winter nights mean this book is literally set in darkness.

We get the first appearance of DI Linford, thorn in the side of Rebus and maybe love interest of Siobhan Clarke. It's good to have him around. Rankin has been trying out proper foils for Rebus in the force for years and none have stuck, but Linford is perfect, because he is the antithesis of Rebus: careerist, a suck up, weird. Talking of which we get the first book where it's Clarke (not Siobhan): a conscious switch by Rankin to allow her equal gravitas. She also gets a lead role and takes on the narrative, so surname order is required. DC's Ellen Wylie and Grant Hood make their debuts too. The Garibaldi estate, a fictional shit hole is back from *Mortal Causes* and makes its last appearance.

First use of the phrase 'high hiedyins' referring to the bosses at 'the big house', i.e. police headquarters at Fettes. A "Big high hiedyin" (big high head one) is a comical Scottish expression meaning the man (or woman) in charge: in short, a bigwig.

First time another of Rankin's favourite bars Swany's gets a mention, as do a lot of the Ox's real regulars.

Last reference to Brian Holmes – he's somewhere in Australia. Last mentions of Patience, Vanderhyde, and the bloody Sword and Shield

Background:

Rankin makes a big play of the serendipitous nature of the creation of this story. He says he picked up an in-flight magazine on a book tour in the USA and read about Queensberry house where the opening scenes are set, and the body is discovered. On returning to Scotland he arranged a tour of the House and was present when the fireplace was discovered, although there was no body of course. The scenes describing what was happening there in lieu of the new Parliament building are accurate.

Rankin had just signed a three-book deal and he had the idea of all three featuring a man who would eventually become a member of the Scottish Parliament. In Rankin's words: "(it became) a one-book trilogy. I'd originally thought that within the series I'd create an interlinked trilogy about the new Scottish Parliament. But two things happened. First, I decided that the Scots Parliament only deserved a one-book trilogy - that's plenty for these idiots and second, there was one character who was going to be in all three books, a member of the Parliament - in Book One he's running for Parliament, in Book Two he's elected and in Book Three the Parliament's up and running. But 40 or 50 pages into Book One, the book whispers to me, *Kill him.* I thought: No way, I've got three mysteries I'm working on, I don't need this hassle. *No*, said the book, *you've got to kill him. He's got to go.* Well, books have got an internal logic and there's fuck-all you can do about it. So I killed the guy. And once he got bumped off, sure enough, I felt a lot more comfortable with the book. Of course, I didn't know who killed him, I didn't know why he died - I just had an extra corpse on my hands. The book told me what to do and I went along with it. It was the right decision, even if it did mean an end to my plans for a trilogy."

This an interesting view of Rankin's about Scotland at the time. It comes from an interview he gave J. Kingston Pierce for *January* magazine (a Canadian publication) in 2000. Since then the rise of the Scottish National Party (SNP) has created a real enthusiasm for Scottish politics and independence as a possible concept. Few would call the Scottish Parliament idiots (at the time of writing). As we write the United Kingdom as we have known it for 300 years is hanging by a thread, but the English part of us warns the Scottish part of us that Scottish history is littered with stories of Scottish hopes dashed and expectations crushed. It'll end in tears. Rankin in 2014 has a slightly different view but avoided

105

publishing a new Rebus book at the time of the 2014 Referendum on independence ('Yes' lost by 55% to 45%) so that Rebus's world wouldn't be messed up by the result which was due around the time a Rebus book is usually published.

As noted the title comes partly from a poem but also the setting: it's winter in Edinburgh, where it's dark when you go to work and it's dark when you head home. Rankin thought the title worked well, because the new Parliament could be leading Scotland into the light after 300 years of being linked to England. "And Rebus, you know, has his moments of darkness, but always he seems to finally reach a point of light."

Like in *Strip Jack* Rankin creates a fictional Scottish constituency of Edinburgh West End for his made-up MSP Roddy Grieve. For completeness we should note there is an Edinburgh West, which after boundary changes is now Edinburgh Western. It's been a solid Lib Dem seat until 2011, when it went to SNP, and has never been a Labour seat. After the rise of the SNP in 2015 will there ever be a Labour MP in Scotland again?

In truth the skeleton in an old building is another good example of Rankin recycling. It is very similar to the short story from *A Good Hanging* called *Concrete Evidence,* and Rankin even recycles a character from that story to provide some background here.

We should mention Hugh MacDiarmid here. Rankin used a line from a poem of his in his epigraph for *Mortal Causes*. He was born Christopher Murray Grieve - see what he did there – but was known by his pen name. He was a poet. He was instrumental in creating a Scottish version of modernism and was a leading light in the Scottish Renaissance of the 20th century. Much of MacDiarmid's political life, however, was spent advancing the cause of Scottish nationalism and was a founder of the Scottish National Party. The book has a variety of Grieve references: a poem at Roddy Grieve's mother's house and Rebus is able to recognise another line from MacDiarmid at the MSP building, he'd seen it in a book in his recent self-education. MacDiarmid lines also start both parts of *Set in Darkness*.

Anyone growing up in the UK in the 1990s will know where Rankin got the idea about Cafferty's escape from incarceration. It parallels the case of Sir Ernest Saunders, erstwhile Chief Executive of Guinness who was found guilty of manipulating the share price and jailed for five years in 1991. He was released on compassionate grounds because he was apparently suffering the symptoms of Alzheimer's disease - which are irreversible. Upon release he made an apparent full recovery and is still alive in 2015.

More than ever before Rankin builds in places in Edinburgh, real life people and real other places. So we get the fish restaurant, Kim. The Patak is a fine Indian restaurant, not far from Arden St (Trip Advisor gives it 4.5 stars and is middle Ranking by Edinburgh standards). The raisin day prank *did* happen on November 18th of 1998, although Rankin has changed the details completely.

Things That Don't Make Sense:

Rebus is right about the release date of the Rolling Stones album *Some Girls* but you do have to wonder what the dead body was thinking wearing flares post 1978.

The use of computers in that era is also problematic. The operating system DOS wasn't used on computers until 1981 and the chances of anyone really using a word processor in 1980 is virtually impossible, although some archaic examples existed. Word processing in easy form is associated with the Apple Mac around 1983 and early Windows models. Put it this way, if someone like Douglas Adams wasn't using word processors until the mid-eighties then there's no way these nobodies would.

Mrs. Cochrane in Arden St has gone or isn't mentioned, which is equally weird.

We get our usual Siobhan is a DS error on p 308. Talking of Siobhan Rankin cranks up the coincidences, or the small-Edinburgh Village weirdness when Nic and Jerry randomly chat up Siobhan in their car. Siobhan walks away and immediately witnesses a leaper worth £400,000.

Farmer Watson mixes up the words appraise and apprise when he suggests Linford should be appraised of the situation; proof readers these days…

This is dated by Hibernian not being in the Scottish Premier League (1998-1999 season) and the League being on a winter break. This means it must be December 1998, based on it not being Christmas yet in the text. However, the winter break, which was an experiment that lasted for three seasons, was always in January... but it's December definitely.

Rebus plays a David Bowie album containing *The Man Who Sold the World* and *Changes*. Believe it or not's it's very hard to find an album that contains both songs. There was a *Best Of* that was released after this book but that's it…Nirvana's version perhaps revived interest in the former song and Rankin guessed.

This is a really pedantic one but when Rob Grieve and Rebus discuss three-piece bands they don't choose the most convincing ones: Supergrass were a three-piece but hardly earth-shattering and played as a four piece on the road. Massive Attack were more a collective than a three-piece and had guest vocalists. The Manic Street Preachers were a three piece only by perverse stubbornness after their guitarist died. Cream are fine, but not mentioning The Jimi Hendrix Experience, Nirvana and the Jam seems weird for such musos.

The Scottish cheese reference on page 292 is lovely, it's credited to Merry Mac Fun, a Scottish troupe named after a page in the Sunday Post. They appeared at the Edinburgh Fringe festival in the early 1980s. Only Rankin seems to remember them, giving us the reference above in a tweet in August 2014. Given Rebus's antipathy to the Festival you do have to wonder how he would

108

remember such an obscure couplet. Tell you what, we'll do the work here. Rhona must have dragged him along. Ironically Rankin feels the need to reference the *Vile Bodies* nod within the text, which is infinitely more obvious than the whole obscure (and unreferenced) cheese poem here.

Siobhan reads Isla Dewar books; she's slightly out of favour now but at the time she might have been the next big chick lit thing that Catharine Alliot or Jojo Moyes became.

The boundaries for seats in the MSP are further muddied because Linford said Grieve would have been his MSP, but he lives in Dean Village (see *Strip Jack*), which is in the Edinburgh North and Leith constituency: definitely not West End by any stretch of the imagination...

Musical references:

We'll ignore the two fictional bands here of course.

Title page:
Wages Day (lyric excerpt) - Deacon Blue

Rolling Stones references:
Some Girls (LP) - Rolling Stones – on the deceased's T-shirt
Monkey Man - Rolling Stones – a Rebus nickname

Music on the hi-fi
The Blue Nile (unspecified LP) – given to him by Siobhan
The Man Who Sold the World - David Bowie
Changes - David Bowie (but see *Things that don't make sense*)
Changes - Black Sabbath
Blue Valentine (LP) - Tom Waits
White Album - The Beatles – Rebus' New Year's eve listening

Car music
Wishbone Ash – what Rebus apparently listens to on surveillance jobs
Love or Confusion - Jimi Hendrix – but also metaphorical for Rebus's state of mind
(Unspecified LP) - Page & Plant – probably *Walking into Clarksdale*, as it had been recently released

Three piece bands:
Manic Street Preachers, Massive Attack, Supergrass, Cream, Jimi Hendrix experience (see Things That Don't Make Sense)

Siobhan's hi-fi
Belle & Sebastian

Jerry's reminiscences of good tunes:
Your Generation - Generation X
Don't Care - Klark Kent
Where's Captain Kirk? - Spizz Energi
The Ramones
Johnny & The Self-Abusers - Simple Minds
Alex Harvey, Status Quo, Iggy Pop Stranded/No Time - The Saints
(Get a) Grip (on Yourself) - The Stranglers

Gifts
Crime of the Century – Supertramp – Rebus to Siobhan
Walk Across the Rooftops - The Blue Nile – Siobhan to Rebus
Tinseltown in the Rain - The Blue Nile – Siobhan to Rebus
Sundry references:
Barclay James Harvest – an Usher Hall concert in the 1970s where Obscura were also on the bill
Supertramp – nickname of the dead tramp
Woodwork Creaks and Out Come the Freaks - Was (Not Was) – Rebus quotes it

110

Wish You Were Here (LP) - Pink Floyd – Rebus remembering 1975.

Review:

What can we say? It's the best Rebus to date, almost magnificent. After the previous torrid two novels Rankin eases up a bit and gives us a textbook police procedural. The coincidences work brilliantly this time, Cafferty is resurgent and magnificent, Rebus working as a team player and the modern Rebus novel is finally in place. Rankin is great with cold case stuff and doesn't do enough of it. Linford is nasty, Rebus is on fire and Clarke allows this to be better because it stops Rebus being just another private eye.

As is often the case it's the weaknesses that are most interesting, but please don't imply that it makes the book worth any less. The rape storyline could and should have been removed; it has absolutely nothing to do with the main thrust of the story, which is far more interesting. All it does is infuriate critics of Rankin's over-coincidence. Without it it's much leaner.

This is nearly the best Rankin whodunit too, except for the obscure revelations of almost all of the mysteries in this book. Again, this is not a criticism, more a realistic twist on the norms of such books of this genre. In fact there is just so much to enjoy here. The Leith descriptions crackle, and despite us moaning about the 'Rebus alone with cheese on toast in his flat' section, it's simply brilliant.

The New Statesmen in 2000 agreed, calling this the best Rankin to date. "*Set in Darkness* could be the umbrella title of the whole series. Few aspects of contemporary Scotland have escaped Rankin's attention, yet he is neither an issue-based writer nor a crusader; with sparse, clear prose and a refusal to overdramatize, he describes social realities from homelessness to political corruption in a way that highlights convincingly - and movingly - the levels of despair to be found in each. In Rebus's world, the crime is the least

111

important of the problems to be solved; invariably, it is the only one that ever finds an answer. That refusal to simplify, to restore order at all costs, makes Rankin a writer who has shown just how far the boundaries of crime fiction can be stretched."

No surprise this won the 2005 Grand Prix du Roman Policier which Rankin was amused by, because he couldn't find a French publisher while he lived in France.

The Falls

Published by: Orion (2001)

One line summary: Rebus finds himself reliving the plot of the film *Chinatown*, whilst Siobhan recreates the TV show *Treasure Hunt*, without the jumpsuit.

Cover: The first edition has a rather large waterfall on the cover. It's a weir on the water of Leith. The latest version has another giant waterfall on the cover. The American cover has a doll's face on it that in no way resembles the dolls in the story: could do better cover designers.

TV Adaptation:
The first in the Ken Stott rebooted series. It's fair to give a nod to the re-boot at this point. They make the mistake of trying to squeeze the huge Rankin plots into one hour leaving only the faintest traces of the original books. Stott looks right and sounds right to many fans, certainly more than John Hannah, but still isn't right for the authors of this book, and although the series had its fans it never became as popular as other TV detectives. Possibly this was because Rankin wasn't keen on them developing new stories, either way he has now bought the rights back, so no more stories can be made.

It was also the first of the Radio adaptations in 2008 starring Ron Donachie.

Four things to notice about The Falls:

1) We're finally into the Rebus 'doesn't get any' era of the books, although ironically he does in this book but it's the last time. Rebus laments the condom packet with one left, well past its sell-by-date. Given that sell-by-dates on prophylactics are often five years, this is almost impressive.

It's hard therefore to believe that this is the same man who slept with one of the great (fictional) iconic fashion models of the 1970s in the previous book! Of course he does form a relationship with Jean Burchill here and it's still going after this book, but not for long and the die is cast: Rankin isn't really interested in Rebus's love interests. In an interview once he noted that Miranda often vetoed characters, including Patience by pointing out how boring they are – and it's true. And for further proof look at how unattached the other major character, Siobhan is, although, Rankin defends this in interviews, saying the books take up ten days and she could be partying for the other 350 days of the year.

2) We're also into the classic era of nicknames, with Tommy Daniels getting saddled with 'Distant' (via Tom Tom to drums to Jim Reeves' *Distant Drums*) being the best one yet.

3) Rankin lets Rebus admit to the same cobbles/setts error he made in *Hide and Seek*. This is significant because it coincides with Rankin's fan base being large enough to have people correct his continuity for him and offer to keep an eye on it. From this book onward you get a lot more references/ corrections to the past. Before this it seemed Rankin didn't care particularly.

4) Rankin previews the title of the next book in the series when he uses the phrase Resurrection Men, a reference to Burke and Hare and tangential to the plot in this book. It wasn't intentional per se, more that he found the phrase, liked it and thought, that's going to be the title of the next book. As we shall see the next book came to Rankin so completely it must have been almost a frustration to finish this one and get on with the one he really wanted to write...

Firsts and Lasts:

Rankin's - at the time - favourite new band, Mogwai make their first appearance via Siobhan, and in the credits. They will be essential to the plot of the next book but one too. They are one of the greatest Scottish bands. Go to iTunes now...

Most important and obvious is this is the last appearance of Farmer Watson, as the action effectively starts at his retirement do. He'll be missed and never adequately replaced, despite Gill Templer making a good fist of it.

First reference to HOLMES: the Home Office Large Major Enquiry System, a computerized database of information on crimes nationwide. It's actually HOLMES 2 though; the original HOLMES had been around since the mid-1980s, but it wasn't very good. HOLMES 2 was a vast improvement, which is a bit of a shame because it wasn't released to police forces until 2000, so if this set a few months after *Set in Darkness* (as is implied by the text) then it wasn't in existence then. Oh, and ironically it's also the last appearance of HOLMES! It's also the first time the internet really becomes a big deal in the series (obvs).

First appearance of nasty journalist Steve Holly, taking on the Jim Stevens role. It's the last and only latter day book up to retirement to have no Cafferty references at all. This was deliberate by Rankin.

And it's the first time Siobhan gets equal billing...

Background:

Rankin knew the title before he had the idea for the book. He was in New Zealand and heard a song by the Mutton Birds on an advert and bought the CD *Rain, Steam and Speed* at the airport on a whim. Listening to it back in Edinburgh he was taken by the track *The Falls* and its haunting lyrics. A few days later (as Rankin tells it) he was making a documentary for a French TV station and suggested the recently opened Museum of Scotland would make a good backdrop. On arrival a member of staff saw the famous author and thought he'd like a look at the little dolls on the Fourth Floor. A few weeks later Rankin did so, because it nagged at him that he'd never heard of them. It was then that he made his first encounter with the Arthur's Seat dolls and coffins, which were found in 1836 and a cornerstone of the book. So impressed was Rankin by the museum, and presumably the coffins that he created the character of Jean Burchill, Rebus latest lover, who was a curator at this very museum.

Rankin liked the coffins because nobody had a satisfactory answer to the question of who made them and why. He also liked the idea that he could fill in the gaps. He even surpassed himself (or perhaps shot himself in the foot) by creating from scratch the marvellous and very plausible character of Kennet Lovell, who seems so real…let's say people researching Rankin um spent a lot of time fruitlessly searching for information about him!

Once Rankin had the idea of a waterfall from the Mutton Birds, and weird mysteries as a theme for this book he dived into his green folder to find another weird, unsolved mystery from the recent past to bolster up the page count. The one that intrigued him most was the case of Frenchman Emmanuel Caillet, whose body was found on Ben Alder in June 1996. He had been dead for months, killed by a gun of some sort, way off the beaten track. His credit cards were gone, all labels cut out of his clothes. He was also carrying an old Remington .44 gun, a sleeping bag but no tent, non-walking shoes and lots of water, even though Scotland is a very wet place. The police concluded he came to commit suicide. He wasn't formally identified until a year later when police reconstructed his visage from the skull. He had left France with camping gear in August 1995 to holiday in London. He disappeared immediately after checking in to a hotel in Glasgow and never used credit cards or bank accounts again. The pathologist (a certain Dr Rankin would you believe!) insisted that Caillet killed himself. However he was seen in his last days with a mysterious and controlling olive skinned-man and wild rumours of him being in some kind of role playing game/ society never went away. Rankin took this story and ran with it, creating a different version with a German tourist, and making Flip Balfour become involved with an on-line game too: Rankin acknowledges the lift in the afterword but gets the father's profession wrong. He also 'fesses up to Kennet Lowell. John Rebus would have had no skills in an online game solving storyline so Siobhan needed to be promoted to co-star to lead this part of the investigation. This will lead to her promotion in the next book.

Things That Don't Make Sense:

Given the description of the waterfall in the text isn't the waterfall on the original cover a little spectacular?

Falls as a town is fictional but you have to ask why Rankin bothers to mention its twin town Angoisse (which means anguish), which is in the Dordogne region in France. If you've been reading, you work it out!

There are superficial similarities to the plot of *Chinatown,* which we won't go into, but it's there; we think it's coincidence, although Rankin does cite the film as one of his inspirations, along with *The Maltese Falcon*, even as late as 2013.

Dating this story is problematic. The book was released in 2001 but it's stated in the text that it's a 'few' months after the events of *Set in Darkness*. As that was definitely in early 1999, this must be set in late Spring 1999, which if true buggers up the time frame (as ever). For example, the Lou Reed concert mentioned in the text is probably meant to mimic the real Lou Reed concert at the Edinburgh Playhouse May 17th 2000. The other dating problem is that Rankin mentions the glorious headline in the Scottish Sun newspaper that coincided with a giant killing football result. Inverness Caledonian Thistle beat Celtic and the headline (a pun-lovers delight) was 'Super Caley go ballistic Celtic are atrocious' was made for Rankin (remember the squid joke). Unfortunately the match was in February 2000! So despite what Rankin writes in his books this book is set when he wrote it – Spring 2000.

We get classic Rankin football errors again. Here he makes a big deal of the TV cameras being at a game, yet they were present at *every* game by 2000. Even the internet joke about the Milan goalie is iffy, although it's funny. It's Inter or Internazionale, never Inter Milan.

Rankin or Rebus in POV is still calling women police officers WPC's, although this went out of use in 2000. We'll just let it go despite the timeline issues.

Even Jean Burchill knows Rebus isn't a drinker, as in an alcoholic.

When the killer starts humming *Sweet Low Sweet Chariot* he says to the victim, "What do you do...when the chariot won't swing low enough," which is a line from, you've guessed it, Rankin's current faves- The Mutton Birds! There is no way the killer would know this band.

Rebus couldn't do a free mason handshake in earlier books, but now he claims that his father taught him how do fake one.

Musical references:

The title, as mentioned is a track by The Mutton Birds. Rankin adds another reference to their Envy of Angels CD later in the text.

Sundry
Wages Day - Deacon Blue – Rebus settles an argument over which album it was on. Not sure Deacon Blue are very Rebusy.
Promised You a Miracle - Simple Minds

CD's owned by Costello
John Martyn, Nick Drake, Joni Mitchell

Hi-fi songs
Beggars Banquet - Rolling Stone
Desire - Bob Dylan, specifically the first track *Hurricane*
Walk on the Wild Side - Lou Reed, which provides a mention of
Grandad - Clive Dunn (composed session bassist Herbie Flowers
who also played on *Walk on the Wild Side*)
Buried Alive in the Blues - Janis Joplin
The Hard Way - Steve Earle

Car songs (including Jean Burchill's)

In Search of Space - Hawkwind
Unspecified - Cream, Rolling Stones
Electric Ladyland - Jimi Hendrix
Burning of the Midnight Lamp - Jimi Hendrix

Reminisces about 1982

Beautiful Vision – especially the track *Dweller on the Threshold* -
Van Morrison

Joke on the word undertone
Teenage Kicks - Undertones

Thought about to express an emotion
Comfortably Numb - Pink Floyd
Bell Boy - The Who – in a lift
Ashes to Ashes - David Bowie
Spider and the Fly B side to Satisfaction - Rolling Stones
A Better Land - Oblivion Express

Concerts
Lou Reed

The last time Rebus was at the Playhouse - UB40
The Fall – of course

Booze deaths
The Faith Healer - Sensational Alex Harvey Band.

Oh, and one of the characters is called Declan McManus (real name of Elvis Costello).

In a rare moment Rankin thanks Mogwai whose *Stanley Kubrick* EP was playing in the background as he wrote *The Falls*), although Siobhan is the one listening to Mogwai most in the book.

Review:

Rankin's methods of working are well known by now: picking up clippings of interesting stories and waiting for an idea to trigger. Never has this been more telegraphed than here with the Caillet case, the Arthur's seat coffins and the new gaming world of the Internet. It has to be said that Rankin doesn't show much real interest in the internet gaming shown here; his clues being more a cross between good cryptic crossword clues and the sort of clue you used to get on the old *3,2,1* show.

The problem here is that the merging the three very disparate worlds creates a horrible mess. The chances of an coffin-leaving serial killer not being noted for thirty years is hard enough to swallow, but just about ok - the chances that they live in the same block as the killer of another girl where a coffin is left is crazy. Now add a third person, entirely unrelated who just happens to make a coffin for publicity purposes takes things too far. So this is a series with a great mystery at it centre that has a series of mundane or irritating resolutions.

Look, it's not a *bad* book but it's not Rankin's best either, and is the weakest of the mid-period books by some distance. Even

Rebus drinking heavily doesn't give it an edge. It's not the lack of Cafferty either, just that there isn't much tension and it doesn't help its cause being sandwiched between two bone fide classics. The points of view change too often too and the story gets lost because of it. At times *nobody* is narrating and Rankin is telling the story almost himself, like a Victorian author. The denouement is prosaic and not very clever, and the other stuff is so wildly unlikely as to make you almost throw the book down. We've read this book three times now: once when it was released, again a few years ago, and thirdly for this book and our opinion is consistent. Fortunately we're about to be blown away by the next one...

It does get its own legendary line though: as Rebus and Jean stare out over the Edinburgh skyline Rebus notes: 'this wasn't a view but a crime scene waiting to happen.'

Resurrection Men

Published by: Orion 2002

One Line summary: Rebus goes back to school to learn how to be a team player with a bunch of other cops who make him look like an angel.

TV Adaptation: Yes, least said the better. It's the first episode of the last series. The essence is there but the plot is squeezed a bit. There was also a radio adaptation in 2008.

Cover: A Templar gravestone from the village of Temple.

Four things to notice about Resurrection Men

1) This contains Rankin's favourite description of Siobhan: Cafferty tells her: "You've got more balls than Tynecastle." "She wouldn't be flattered by that remark," says Rankin, "because it implies she's put her womanness aside to become one of the boys. But it says a lot about her because she's a ballsy character." It adds the added piquancy of being about Heart of Midlothian, not Hibernian too. Cafferty, despite his surname preferring the protestant team. While we're on the subject of great lines, 'Siobhan squeezed out a smile thinner that a prison roll-up,' is also up there with the best.
2) We've alluded to art themes before but here is the first time we notice how knowledgeable and interested in modern art Rankin is. Art is a recurring theme with Rankin and he goes back to it often: two short stories, this story, *Exit Music* and *Doors Open* all have modern art at its core.
3) We get a new understanding of the Arden St flat via *The South Bank Show.* Presented by Melvyn Bragg this was a

long-running and highly respected Arts documentary programme dedicated to showcasing writers, artists, musicians, and actors. Rankin's show allowed him to finally visit Arden St and look around the flat, which was owned by a German lecturer at the university. This gave him the opportunity to get the subtle details right and also excuse the previous omissions. He credits this with the more detailed description of the flat seen here. He even offers us an ironic apology when Jazz McCulloch comments on the decoration in the 'nice stairwell' that Rebus 'hadn't noticed in years' and Rankin of course never knew about.

4) This won the Edgar Award, given by the Mystery Writers of America. Named after Edgar Allen Poe, it would have been the most prestigious award Rankin had won so far. It went one step further than the merely nominated *Black and Blue* and in the future *Saints of the Shadow Bible* (pipped by Stephen King's *Mr. Mercedes*), and richly deserved it. It must have been a bit discombobulating for Rankin though, as he had just finished the first draft of *Fleshmarket Close* at the time, which is two years and one book away from *Resurrection Men.*

Firsts and Lasts:

It's the first title since *The Black Book* to be quite literal, and not a quote, nor a pun nor a song title. First case in a while to use fictionalized crimes after the real ones that kicked off the previous few books. Siobhan is now a DS after a few typographic false starts. First Latin quote: Durate et vosmet **Rebus** servate secundis – 'carry on and preserve yourself for better times.' That's about it!

Background:

Rankin came up with the title while writing *The Falls.* During his research into Burke and Hare and the body snatchers he came across the phrase Resurrection Men in context and liked it so much he knew it would be the title of his next book. Rankin wrote this quickly, the words flying onto the page, he was even writing it during the publicity for *The Falls.*

The plot threads came together rather organically as usual. Another facet was a review of *The Falls* by the Chief Constable of Lothian and Borders Roy Cameron, who had built up quite a habit of writing fairly obvious book reviews in the *Edinburgh Evening News*. His reviews continuously refer to Rebus's drinking and he had started to have some concerns about Siobhan's lifestyle choices too. His review of *The Falls* lamented how he wished he had just one officer like Rebus, which is a bit strong, but added a 'final caveat' that Rebus would have to be sent back to Police College. Rankin wrote to Cameron and arranged a visit to Tulliallan, the College that features heavily in *Resurrection Men*. There Rankin observed training sessions, making notes to add colour. The parachute jump mentioned in the text actually happened. He was particularly taken with the reenactment of a case using trainers to pass on information and let the trainees work the case. When you already had a title like *Resurrection Men* it was pretty obvious what these trainees were going to be like.

The art subplot had been brewing for a few years too. As we've seen Rankin has quite an interest in fine art, (see *Monstrous Trumpet*) especially modern art and although we have no idea when he wrote *Herbert in Motion* (in the *Beggar's Banquet* short story compilation released after this, it's worth a guess that it was written around the time this was being conceived. So adding the art world was logical. Rankin, art fan that he is, created a Vettriano painting for the book, but decided to check that the artist (a Fifer) was happy with the idea. Yeah right, he wasn't being a fanboy, oh no.

Siobhan's car crash also happened to Rankin's in the same place.

Things That Don't Make Sense:

At Tulliallen Tennant tells the Resurrection Men how they trained to be CID back in the day. They were "videotaped." We doubt that was true given the ages of these men when they would have gone for CID. Rankin is guilty feeding us the research he did when he was there.

Rebus claims his car is 14 years old, which takes us rather conveniently back to the published date of *Knots and Crosses*. Now we all know that Rankin enjoys being deliberately obtuse when discussing the Saab but as it's hard to believe Rebus bought the car new in 1987, and it seems to have been arthritic even in the early books. One has to assume the Saab is a later purchase, which Rankin seems to have forgotten to mention. Our favourite theory is that he bought Gregor Jack's Saab.

Rankin is still calling female police officers WPC's although the title was officially dropped in 2000/2001.

Siobhan recalls run ins with Cafferty. Has she ever met him?

Musical references:

Preface
All men have secrets... What Difference Does it Make? The Smiths

Came up in conversation
Tristan und Isolde (Wagner)

Phone ring tone
Mission Impossible Theme

Car music

Steely Dan, Morphine, Neil Young, Van Morrison, John Martyn
Curved air, Fairport Convention

Rebus's hi-fi
Immigrant Song - Led Zeppelin
Exile on Main Street - Rolling Stones
Montrose – Montrose
Jackie Leven
Bad Company - Bad Company
Saint Dominic's Preview - Van Morrison
(Unspecified LP) – Mogwai (although Siobhan put it on)
(Unspecified LP) - The Blue Nile
Us - Sparks
Physical Graffiti - Led Zeppelin

Turn of phrase
Career Opportunities - The Clash
Fun House (LP) - The Stooges
Four in the Morning - Faron Young – Siobhan waits in casualty, but
can't remember Faron's name.
This Town Ain't Big Enough for the Both of us - Sparks

Siobhan's car
Out of Time – REM

LP not even a thief would steal from Rebus's flat
Nazareth

Tape made for Rebus by Siobhan
(Unspecified LP) - Arab Strap

Siobhan's taste
Rock Action - Mogwai
Hobotalk
Goldfrapp

Siobhan's' car
REM
Boards of Canada

Also Mentioned
Slipknot – assumption of the type of music played by students.
Cocteau Twins who came from Grangemouth, which is between
Edinburgh and Tulliallan and the oil refinery was a clear landmark
on Rebus's journeys to and fro.
Travis t-shirt Alan Ward wears to bed

Review:

We must declare an interest here, this is our favourite Rankin. It's
breathtaking from page one. The rather obvious opening that is
deliberately designed to fool us and everyone in the book. We
expect Rebus to be in trouble, although eventually Rankin plays so
fair and he tells the audience it's an act. It's still a master stroke.
Outside of Rebus's shenanigans this is also makes Siobhan the star
of the show and she does great work interacting with Cafferty, who
also raises the quality of the book simply by being in it.

It won awards and it's easy to see why, as it pits the ever
morally ambiguous Rebus in with some genuinely bent coppers,
which makes us realise how moral our hero actually is, despite the
fact that in Rebus's world everyone assumes he's bent, or in the
pocket of Cafferty. The cold-case scenes crackle, as Rebus and Gray
size each other up and decide it's a score draw. The problem
perhaps with hindsight is that Rankin could have played us along a

little longer, but he lets us know too soon. In addition the murder of the art dealer doesn't go far enough and the linking theme to the whole thing is ridiculously contrived. Is there actually a reason why the normal case used in these sessions has been changed for example? So we have a book which has all the style and swagger of a great mid-to-late period Rankin but it doesn't quite have the substance, but if you're reading it for the first time you don't notice because the power of the premise just keeps you gripped.

Why is this so good? Because Rebus fits into the story and Rankin keeps just enough from us to reel us in. In truth the characters and the style is not far off his mid period stuff like *Let it Bleed* but with the stakes raised to ten and a whole room of policemen who are interesting enough to have a series written about them this is simply a winner.

Beggar's Banquet

Beggar's Banquet is a much better collection than *A Good Hanging and other Stories*, which had a contractual obligation feel about it. The truth is that although this book you're reading is about John Rebus we recommend the other stories here too, especially *Herbert in Motion*, the art heist one, which has links to many other stories. The dates were confirmed in the 2014 compilation *The Beat Goes On*. We're pleased at how close our guesses were!

Trip Trap (1992)

We date it to the mid-nineties because Rebus is choosing jazz to listen to and Patience and Rebus are a few years into their relationship. We could have done without the thought of Patience going commando but it's a nice story nevertheless, although a better twist would have been for the 'crime' to be an accident, rather than the obvious, although the word play is delightful.

Facing the Music (1994)

Rebus acts weirdly, seemingly condoning a theft from a hi-fi shop that allows Rankin to write about expensive kit again. It's actually quite a nice story but, as usual the best fun is trying to date it. Pre-knowing the Saab is a Saab and with Rebus just starting to be a Stones fan we'd say between *Mortal Causes* and *Let it Bleed*, which would be appropriate, as that's the album he wants to hear on the 25thou turntable. It is of course also the album he used to test systems in his hi fi review days.

Talk show (1991)

Rebus solves a crank caller at a radio station case in one of our favourite short stories; here Rebus barely a police officer, more a private eye. Dating is tricky, as Rebus is aged around 44 but single and shagging, so pre-Patience? The dates don't add up (again) *Strip Jack* era is the best bet, if he and Patience were on a break, but it's still difficult to explain why he listens to Radio 3 in the car.

Castle Dangerous (1993)

A full British tour for Americans that doesn't include Oxford: come on! Light-hearted and probably worth a full outing if Rankin had wanted it - Colin Dexter made a whole book out of a similar tale. Difficult to place (as usual). The Farmer is a Superintendent and the police doctor isn't Gates or Curt.

In the Frame (1992)

Another story where the premise is good enough for a lesser writer to use for a whole story. The way Rankin uses it and the mistaken identity makes this a far jollier story than it probably deserves, but this is still one of the better Rebus short stories.

No Sanity Clause (2000)

Definitely dated after *The Falls* as MSPs mentioned and Jean Burchill is Rebus' girlfriend. The reference to Rebus asking for a CD by String Driven Thing is classic Rankin going super obscure. Look them up. This was written for this collection and a bit flimsy, although it's a great idea pulled about to give it some body. It fulfils Rankin's desire for tautness with a short word count.

Window of Opportunity

Weird one because this must be set in an alternative Rebus universe where we meet two DC's we've never met before and Rebus's boss doesn't get a name. Nice little tale, if a little soft in its approach to crime: more Ealing comedy if you like.

Review:

You rarely get a bad Rankin short story and there are some crackers here. Some are lighthearted and some are frustratingly short, you just want to keep reading about Rebus and Edinburgh, so this is more a frustrating collection and the tone is more even than the previous, which is a shame. We needed just a little more darkness.

A Question of Blood

Published by: Orion (2003)

One line Summary: The title says it all: a horrific shooting incident at a private school forces Rebus to come to terms with the ties of family and friends and how some people just don't fit in.

TV adaptation: The second episode of Ken Stott's second series.

Cover: Port Edgar marina, South Queensferry, where the action is set.

Five things to notice about A Question of Blood:

1) The 'ambiguous Rebus motive' plot strand is becoming a bit of a cliché after the layers of Rebus ambiguity in *Resurrection Men*. In that book there were at least three things Rankin was keeping from the reader and here, on page one we have another, with Rebus being vague about his burnt hands and Siobhan's stalker dead in a fire. Rankin returns to this ambiguous Rebus to a lesser extent in *Saints of the Shadow Bible*.

2) The Siobhan/Rebus 'tension' reaches its zenith here. There's the obvious end scene of course, but throughout the book Siobhan is forced to look after the disabled Rebus, whose burnt arms prevent him from picking up a pint glass or lighting a cigarette. For the first time there are hints of jealousy/flirtation, especially when Siobhan mentions that Rebus's old mate Bobby Hogan asked her out. Rankin cools it off after this book, which is the right call, but he has noted in various interviews that there could have been romance. He also gave brief thought to Siobhan being gay: a Hibernian-supporting, short-haired police officer being lesbian wouldn't be a surprise.

132

In truth perhaps the only flaw in the character of Siobhan Clarke is her lack of interest in sex: it's the only thing that doesn't ring true.

3) Siobhan and Rebus are listening to a song in the car but don't mention what song it is. It's *Drop the Hate* by Fatboy Slim (boy, did that take some research from the obscure clue in the book!) and Rebus mishears the lyrics. It brings up one of the dated aspects of the Rebus books. It's well established by this stage that Rebus is the man who listens to traditional rock music. Siobhan listens to the new and trendy stuff. Sadly most of the modern music Siobhan listens to hasn't lasted the test of time at all, whereas Rebus's stuff still stands out as great. The top three all-time Scottish artists lists in this book however are similarly dated. Does anybody listen to Travis anymore?

4) One of auxiliary character's names is, as usual, a charity auction winner. At a London auction the winner told Rankin, "I don't mind what kind of character I am as long as my mate Wee Evil Bob can be mentioned as well." The winner gave Rankin the name Peacock Johnson. Rankin had such fun creating and writing the characters Peacock Johnson and Evil Bob into *A Question of Blood* that he tried to contact Johnson to ask if he could include them in other novels. He found that the website and the email address he had been given didn't exist, and after doing some sleuthing of his own, Rankin discovered he was the target of a practical joke by Stuart David, the former bass player for the band Belle and Sebastian. Stuart David revealed that Peacock Johnson is a character in two of his own novels. "I thought I'd taken a real man and made him fiction," says Rankin, "but I'd actually taken a fictional man and made him fictional." It also explains how weird the character is. We had him pinned down as our first ethnic minority in the series who isn't working in an Indian

restaurant, but he isn't (we think) see *Fleshmarket Close*. Judging by Peacock's Twitter account he's white. Yes, we say that again, Peacock has a Twitter account.

5) Rebus line at the hospital about 'dribbling dirt trousers' is a reference to escaping concentration camps. Despite *The Hanging Garden* not getting translated into German because of the nature of the material this line was translated by his German publisher. This was probably because Rankin explained the joke in a live reading in German in Germany and it went down well.

First and Lasts:

It's the last time we have a title that isn't a quote or a song title, or a place. It's also the last good old fashioned punning title. Also, the last time we're based at St Leonard's, it even gets an RIP in the credits. This also means we say goodbye to St Leonard's regulars Gill Templer and a few of the other old St Leonard's faces, like DCI Bill Pryde, Hi Ho Silvers. It's also the last appearance of ACC (Crime) Colin Carswell - all haircut and eau de Cologne, which means the last mention of his lap dog DI Linford. Last physical appearance of Bobby Hogan, although we hear about him later on. First appearance in a while of DC 'Rat Arse' Reynolds, who goes by the first name 'Charlie' in this book…now go forward to *Exit Music*. First mention of The Complaints, the internal investigation team who will be a focus of later Rankin books. It's the first time Rebus uses the internet at his flat.

Background:

Rankin says the impetus for this book was a fan question at a 'meet the author' event concerning why he had never written about the private school system in Edinburgh. Firstly, for American viewers, in the UK we call fee-paying schools private schools, or confusingly, public schools. Regular high schools are called state schools. (One of the authors must declare an interest here, as he works in the one of the UK's top fee paying public schools.) Rankin gave a glib answer at the time, that he didn't know about these type of schools, having never been to one, which is a fair point (see Things That Don't Make Sense), but later Rankin got thinking and did some research; he acknowledged the unusually high number of Edinburgh students who attended fee paying schools. The Prime Minister at the time, Tony Blair had attended the very Independent Fettes College in Edinburgh, near the police headquarters, and remember this was before the Eton College mafia took over British society, led by David Cameron and Boris Johnson. That was in 2010 and perhaps indirectly led to the rise of the SNP in recent times. Rankin found the private/state school difference gave him another Jekyll and Hyde analogy again. He decided to set the school outside of the city so that he wouldn't be accused of writing about a real school. This gave him the opportunity to look at how small communities respond to tragedy.

Rankin explains: "A lot of soldiers came back from the first Gulf War changed men. Wife beaters, murderers, and some suicide cases. Part of the book is about this. How the army trains men to kill, and then sends them back home without switching them off.

"But I also had this general theme of outsiders and the periphery of society: teenagers who don't want to fit in, they take to the extremes just to be different; other people like these disaffected soldiers; and even Rebus himself. I wanted to look at how these people are viewed."

Given that Rankin was keen to write about outsiders it didn't take him long to think of returning army vets and their problems, which led to gun crime and ultimately the Dunblane shootings, although Rankin was definitely not writing about that. This meant that *A Question of Blood* created newspaper fuss with only a few chapters written when Rankin revealed at the Edinburgh Book Festival that it began with a shooting at a Scottish school. He was accused of 'ghoulishly fictionalizing' the Dunblane tragedy that happened in 1996...he wasn't.

Once he had the whole outsider think licked it was easy to add teen group de jour, the Goth to the mix. They deliberately eschew others, celebrate being outsiders, despite their dress code being paradoxically strict and highly visible. The line, 'Can't you walk like human beings?' related to the Goths in the book actually happened to Rankin as a kid on the same street where it happened in the book, although of course Rankin wasn't a goth. "The music is a good shorthand way to delineate character," Rankin says. "If you want to tell the reader a lot about a character in a small space, just tell them what their musical taste is. You'll get their age, their background, whether they're gregarious or a loner." The same can also be applied to a skinhead, a punk or a goth and their fashions, and Rankin does that here.

Rankin also wanted to explore family ties and how strong they can be, hence the title. Rebus is personally involved here too, which would be an absolute no-no in real life, but the added layering makes this so much better. As *The Guardian* said on release: "It's apparent, too, in the title's pun. A case that turns on blood-spattered diagrams also brings Rebus up against his own red stuff. One of the students killed in the school tragedy is his cousin's kid. Because of this - and the fact that the college gunman is, like Rebus, ex-army - the detective is forced to construct a psychological profile of himself: a man with a lost daughter, distant friends and a pale, loner lifestyle." This is perfectly summarised in the heartbreaking story of Rebus's cruelty to Allan Renshaw as kid, which Rebus does not remember and has a completely different, happy memory.

Add this to the mix the Jura air crash story from the green folder, which happened in 1994 and was still a bit of a mystery, which fitted in with Rebus's army background and the story was taking shape.

Although we'll write about the ambiguity of how Rebus got his burns and the fact that he has to rely on Siobhan much more here, it's also a welcome reminder that Rebus's time was nearly up. Rankin had made the call to age Rebus in real time so he knew he was going to need to do something about it soon. In Siobhan he had a natural replacement and the helpless Rebus here is a subtle way of starting the process of handing over the reins by making her look like the strong one. There are strong clues in *A Question of Blood* that Rankin is contemplating a successor. Indeed, there was speculation at the time that the unresolved sexual tension between Rebus and Clarke showed that she was a shoe-in. Back to the Guardian: "this novel raises the possibility that Rebus may yet become a Denis Thatcher of crime fiction, pouring whiskeys (sic) for the new premier character and chatting over the plots."

Other winners of auctions to get their name in the book included the owner of a cat who wanted, yep, their cat to be in the book: Boethius we salute you. Also, Brendan Innes an Australian serving police officer became...an Australian serving police officer, who, according to the a line in the book, Rebus never got round to asking what he was doing in Edinburgh (but see Things don't make sense).

Things That Don't Make Sense:

Rankin was right to be reluctant to write about public schools. He doesn't know much about them. He goes for old buildings and snobbery, but public schools rarely have Senior Common Rooms as described, areas are much more likely to be divided by Houses.

Casting our mind back, could you just plug in a computer for example at Rebus's un-networked flat and access the internet in 2002?

Rankin clearly states in his introduction to the 2006 reprint that he had to stress to auction winner Brendan Innes that because it was fiction he couldn't mention his nationality nor his academic credentials (the real Innes, an Australian policeman has a doctorate in astronomy) but Rankin DOES mention his nationality, see the quote we used in the Background section.

We know it's only fiction but Rebus and Siobhan's plane flight to Jura has some timing issues. The conversation they have lasts from Edinburgh to Greenock, which is fine and about half way through the journey, but then the rest of the journey flies by in about two minutes. Also Rankin says the plane is a Cessna and writes about the 'propellers', implying a twin engine, and writes 'engines' once; but Cessna four-seaters only come with a single propeller.

Siobhan claims to have not been out to South Queensferry for years but was in North Queensferry in the last story, which we know are different places and across the water but it's hardly noteworthy, and she must have at least driven 'over' it to get to North Queensferry.

Rebus calls Siobhan DC Clarke on p323, it's becoming cute now that Rankin can't get the ranks right. And while we're at it, and this could be subtle, nuanced characterization by Rankin, but Siobhan has now fully renounced her vegetarianism of the earlier books.

A lot of the tension in this book is of the 'did he, didn't he?' kill Siobhan's stalker type. Given Rebus's excuse that it's a scald and the alleged burns are from a chip pan it must be noted that there would be differences between these two types of injuries based on the huge variation in the temperatures of the fires concerned and the nature of them.

There's some problems with Siobhan's age too but we'll deal with them in *Fleshmarket Close*.

For a novel that contains a goth and an author who loves music there are barely any references to goth music at all. And the top three Scottish acts lists are all terrible, especially Siobhan's and Rebus forgets Jackie Leven.

Musical references:

Mogwai's *Come on Die Young* is a big motif throughout the book.

Common room poster
Eminem

Miss Teri haircut style
Siouxsie Sioux (hairstyle)

Siobhan might start a party with:
Motorhead

CD Rebus plays that Siobhan has given him and he hasn't listened to
Roulette - Violet Indiana

Siobhan's car:
Drop the Hate - Fatboy Slim
Tempus – we must admit we're lost by this reference. Can anyone help? Rebus responds 'fugit'

CDs at Lee Herdman's place
Linkin Park, Sepultura

Boys' jazz taste

Miles Davis, Ornette Coleman, John Coltrane, John Zorn, Thelonious Monk, Archie Shepp

Peacock Johnson's moustache style
Kid Creole

Discussion of top Scottish acts (See Things that don't Make Sense)

Rod Stewart, Big Country, Travis – Siobhan's
Lulu, Annie Lennox - Ray Duff's
Nazareth, Alex Harvey, Deacon Blue –Rebus's , but he continues -
John Martyn, Jack Bruce, Ian Anderson, Donovan, Incredible String
Band, Lulu, Maggie Bell, Simple Minds, Pallas.

Rebus's hi-fi

 Fairytales for Hardmen - Jackie Leven
Anthology – Hawkwind

Ambient music Siobhan is trying to get into
Lemon Jelly, Oldsolar, Boards of Canada, Aphex Twin, Autechre
Rebus's thoughts
I'm A Man - probably the Spencer Davis Group
Another Green World - Brian Eno – the island

Sundry
In Search of Space (LP cover) – Hawkwind
Rolling Stones – Rebus goes off on one about their influence

Rebus's analogies
Rocky Raccoon - The Beatles
Two Out of Three Ain't Bad - Meatloaf

Concert tickets
Foo Fighters, Rammstein, Puddle of Mudd

Initials confusion
The DMC a military section causes some confusion: with Run DMC
and Elton John's record label DJM being mentioned.

Rebus's Car music
Jinx - Rory Gallagher

Review:

It's easy to argue the case that the previous book, *Resurrection Men* is the creative high of the series, but read a decade later looks a little forced. And this follow-up, which at the time reeked of artifice and trendiness, actually stands the test of time far better. Let's be clear *A Question of Blood* is awesome. From the clever pun of the title that flags up the visceral forensics and more importantly, to the theme of family running through this book, it's as if Rankin has just left a big fat clue right there in front of you. Rebus, with his extended family involved in the shooting can find no bond to them and finds his memories of happy days in the past heartbreakingly false. As usual, his own family is found in the Police Force and the ever closer relationship with his colleagues, Siobhan, and Hogan, who is just there to ram the point home. Everybody else is blood-tied and defending it to the hilt, even Siobhan's stalker's family stick together.

This is also one of the most satisfactory Rebus tales, even if the ending is one of Rankin's more famous ambiguous ones, and is more like a sick coda. We would like to know what happened here and we never do, although a certain promotion later in the series suggests the 'nice' possibility.

Rankin, susceptible to panic attacks himself brilliantly describes the gnawing strength-sapping anxiety Siobhan feels in the early chapters. It's as well done as any in popular fiction and not acknowledged often enough.

If you want to be picky the Goth angle is a bit dated, even for 2002; Rankin doesn't really pursue the theme either and we never really feel he gets the scene beyond the superficial and rather obvious point about the clothing. The same goes for the public school theme, which isn't explored at all and any school could have done for the setting of the shooting. Similarly, although we understand the need to paint Rebus black as well as white the whole scalded hand plotline is a contrivance too far (as noted in 'Things that Don't Make Sense' a scald and a burn are very different). And for Rebus to be suspended for seven books in a row seems a bit much. In the hands of a less skilled writer this could have got messy but in Rankin's hands its highly satisfactory and a testament to the great man's skill.

Fleshmarket Close

Published by: Orion (2004)

One-line Summary: A murder of an asylum seeker on a sink-hole estate and a mysterious skeleton found in the cellar of a bar on Fleshmarket Close seem to be linked...

Cover: A moody shot of the Fleshmarket Close street sign. Our favourite.

TV adaptation: Second episode of the first Stott series, although it's a lifeless version.

Four things to Notice about Fleshmarket Close:

1)　　The title came first (according to Rankin). He was walking along Cockburn Street when he saw the sign for Fleshmarket Close, which is a little footpath that leads down to Market Street and the railway station. He liked the name, as it tied in with his thoughts about immigration and the way immigrants and asylum seekers were treated in Scotland. He liked it particularly because, as a fan of the pun, the words Fleshmarket Close suggested a market for bodies is nearby: a Fleshmarket is close. Is that what Scotland was becoming? Fleshmarket Close was the sight of slaughterhouses in the past if you're wondering why it has such a visceral name. The original cover shot has the exact sign that Rankin saw.

2)　　As we will see in the Firsts and Lasts section this book contains the first ethnic minority characters (with dark skin) to appear in the series. We make no comment on this but it's so obvious if you read the books in order that it reminds us of what happened to the producer of the TV series *Midsomer Murders*. In March 2011, producer Brian True-May got caught in an interview talking about the lack of racial diversity in that show. He was reported as saying that if there were ethnic minorities in the show then it wouldn't be *Midsomer Murders* anymore. He was suspended and eventually replaced. The consequences were that a show that was originally set in a mildly fictional idyllic English village setting populated exclusively by indigenous white people, suddenly becomes a show set in a mildly fictional idyllic English village setting populated exclusively by indigenous white people and one person from an ethnic minority. To regular viewers it brings a subtle and amusing extra dimension, as you wait for the token ethnic minority and laugh at how they have shoe-horned them into a regular script written without any ethnic minorities. Our favourite was the man with a broad Jamaican accent, who was a pub landlord and a renowned singer of traditional English folk songs. This has nothing to do with Rankin, who would hate *Midsomer Murders* but he plays it well by highlighting through Rebus the previous lack of diversity before by making Rebus feel guilty that he'd never noticed the immigrant flower sellers before.

3)   Siobhan's age – sigh – we've been avoiding this for some time but lots of things don't add up and in *Fleshmarket Close* the wheels really fall off. Let's try and get a timeline together. We first meet Siobhan in *The Black Book,* where she is a young DC, recently promoted. We shall also assume that this was in 1993, the year the book was published. We also know she was a university graduate, which means that at the youngest she would have been 21 when she joined the force, but with gap years (possibly) she could be up to 23, we'll give Rankin the benefit and assume she was 21. Now, to join CID you need to have done at least a two-year probationary stretch in the woolly suits before you can apply for a trainee position. It doesn't happen automatically and

144

you would be interviewed. Now, assuming Siobhan was on some kind of fast-track graduate scheme she would still need to do the two years so let's make her 23 at the start of *The Black Book*, at the very youngest, but possibly up to 26. Happy so far?

So in *A Question of Blood* Mullen tells Siobhan she could be an Inspector in five years, and a Chief Inspector at 40, but that means her time line is a bit iffy. Remember *A Question of Blood* was set in 2003, which makes Siobhan 33 at the youngest, and 36 at the oldest. Five years is 38 (or 41) and then two years (or -1 years) to be a Chief Inspector? And Mullen seems the sort of person who would know how old Siobhan is.

But it's in this book that we really have a problem. It's 2004, one year after *A Question of blood*. But as we meet the new colleagues at Gayfield Square Siobhan is stated as being 'a few years older than' DC Colin Tibbet, who is in his mid-20s. That kind of implies 29 at the oldest? Which means she was 19 when we met her as a DC? As we've seen in fact Siobhan is at best 34, but could be 37. Essentially Rankin has broken his own rules here because he ages Rebus but seems happy not to age Siobhan, who seems to exist in a permanent state of late 20's early 30-ness.

And things will get really bad in Saints of the Shadow Bible when she is between 43 and 46…but Rankin is still writing her as early thirties.

If you think we're being harsh on this look at this Rankin quote from 2007 about how Siobhan could take over the series: "'I'm thinking about it. Nothing is set in stone, but she's my insurance policy in that she's in her early thirties and therefore has a long career ahead of her (except she is nearer 40 Ian but we'll let it go). I do find her a very interesting character and I think she could carry a series. Partly what put

145

me off until recently is that there is no tradition of men writing well about women in crime fiction."

4) It's worth a trip along Fleshmarket Close to try and work out which bar Rankin was basing The Nook on. The choices are the Jinglin' Geordie or the Halfway House. We go for the Jinglin' Geordie based on the pub sign, the location and the interior, which feels right. It also has a lot of real ale and Rankin would have appreciated it. For British readers the name isn't a reference to people from Newcastle, it's named after local lad George Heriot, he of the university fame.

Firsts and lasts:

First time Gayfield Square is the headquarters of Rebus and Siobhan, so we get to meet DCI James Macrae, DI Derek Starr (who is the station's DI, so Rebus is a spare part), also Colin Tibbet.

If you consider Fleshmarket Close to be a pun then it's the last punning title, otherwise it's the first title named after a place, (although yes, *The Falls* is named after a waterfall). If you're in America this is definitely **not** the last punning title because the book is called *Fleshmarket Alley* there, which makes it the first title to be different to a UK title (*Tooth and Nail* – yes, yes) and by proxy the first title to be named after a road that doesn't exist, and therefore the first really dumb title.

At last, after 14 books we get our first ethnic minority who isn't an Indian waiter. In fact, we get quite a few, because this is about race relations: black dancers, Asian lawyers, black immigration officers, the lot. As we noted above, it reminds us of latter-day *Midsomer Murders*.

First (and last) use of the word 'fuckwittery' - very *Bridget Jones* - a book that had been around for a while, but red hot at the time.

First oblique mention of an iPod, although Rebus doesn't know what one is. First mention of Jackie Leven, who will become a big deal and the last appearance of horrible journalist Steve Holly.

It's the first time Rebus isn't suspended for ages, or the last time he isn't suspended until he retires.

Background:

Verisimilitude, the appearance of truth, is one of the big selling points of Rankin's work over the years. Back in the early 1990s Rankin was marketed as a gritty alternative to the cozy, British detective genre (you know - Christie, Dexter (no relation), Elizabeth George, although she's American writing in the style of British cozy detective fiction). This isn't quite how it worked of course; Rankin simply preferred the American style to British parlour mysteries. One of his ways of convincing *himself* that he was a proper, serious writer was to get the facts right. The police procedure had to be right, the locations became ever more real, the books were set in the present, so real events had to appear (unless it's *Mortal Causes* but that was for sensible reasons). We will argue later that Rankin's break between *Saints of the Shadow Bible* and *Even Dogs in the Wild* was rather convenient because it stopped Rankin having to write about the Scottish Independence Referendum without knowing what the result would be. The vote was in September and a new book is usually delivered in July and published in November.

We're getting ahead of ourselves but this is the book where the verisimilitude comes to bite Rankin on the bum. In the real world St Leonard's police station stopped having a CID division. Rankin tells the story that one of his contacts (a member of CID) sent him a text saying 'St Leonard's hasn't got a CID anymore ha, ha, ha'. This meant he had to move Rebus to another cop shop, and take Siobhan with him (conveniently). The way Rankin tells it he only did it to appease the few dozen knowledgeable readers who would know. He could have played the 'it's fiction' card but chose not to.

But a change is as good as a rest and the Gayfield staff gives a fresh impetus into the series (not that it needed it).

As we've noted already the title came first, but around the same time a charity Rankin worked for called him to tell him about the centre for asylum seekers at Dungavel had only one teacher for all the children in the centre: Dickensian in Rankin's words. He wrote about it in the book as a way of flagging up the problem. Soon after families with kids weren't sent to the Dungavel anymore - they were sent to England instead, which is a very political solution to the problem.

A third strand of serendipitous coincidences was a real-life incident. There was a murder of an asylum seeker on the streets of Glasgow. That made him think a lot about the Scots and about racism and the myth of how welcoming they are to strangers. "We have a big thing going on just now where politicians keep telling us we have a depopulation problem - that the population is going to dip below five million soon and we won't have enough people paying income tax to pay for all the social provisions. So we need immigrants but when they come, they don't get much of a welcome."

"The series as a whole is like a big jigsaw puzzle, I think, and I'm trying to add little bits to the jigsaw. Who are the Scots and what was Scotland like at the end of the 20th century and the beginning of the 21st century? It's part of an ongoing process. There's no big plan for the series. When I get something that's bugging me, some question I want to try to answer, whether it's racism or asylum seekers or paedophiles or war criminals, it could be anything. I just dump everything on Rebus as a way of dealing with it."

Another real-life incident that occurred during the writing of the books was the Morecombe cockling tragedy of 5th February 2004. Morecombe is an English seaside town with a huge bay and treacherous tides. On this day 21 Chinese illegal immigrants lost their lives when a freak tide caught them out. The incident really highlighted the plight of immigrants in the UK and was a huge news story. Newshound Rankin, writing a book about this very thing and one month into the process wouldn't have been able to resist adding it to the book, and he does.

One final thing: Banehall estate is fictional and consistent with Rankin never using real shit holes in his books.

Things That Don't Make Sense:

We've covered a lot of the weird stuff already, but there's a couple more. Siobhan mentions the supermarket Safeway, which didn't exist at the time and had been taken over by Morrisions. Also, it doesn't make sense that Kate, the only Senegalese at the university is also working in the Nook lap dancing club. And how long would someone who doesn't 'do' anything last in such places? Rankin doesn't necessarily play fair here by not describing her clearly in the film, when a black girl in a local amateur porn film might be noteworthy and would be very recognizable.

Musical references:

Siobhan's hi-fi

Felt Mountain - Goldfrapp (although it's credited as their first album in the text)
John Martyn (leant to her by Rebus)
Siobhan's car
Jackie Leven (birthday present to Siobhan from Rebus)

Phrases
Nice Dream – Radiohead: "Nice dream", as Thom Yorke would say.
Son of my Father - Chicory Tip
5.15 - The Who

Old, rubbish song Rebus hums in the morning to get in the head of other people
Wichita Lineman

Ellen Wylie's car music
Norah Jones, Beastie Boys, Mariah Carey

Rebus's hi-fi – potentially and actually
Jackie Leven, Lou Reed, John Mayall's Bluesbreakers (new additions)
Final Straw - Snow Patrol, Virginia Creeper - Grant Lee Phillips (CDs loaned to Rebus by Siobhan)
Dick Gaughan (possibly Rebus' most obscure listen)
Rock 'n' Roll Circus (Video actually)
Montrose, Blue Oyster Cult, Rush, Alex Harvey (LP's he hadn't played in ages)
Goat's Head Soup - Rolling Stones - remembering Ian Stewart
Hard Nose the Highway - Van Morrison
Presumably Beauty in Madness - Hobotalk
Presumably Moving up Country - James Yorkston

Sundry
Albatross - Fleetwood Mac (name of bar in Falkirk)
Brain Salad Surgery (LP cover) - Emerson Lake and Palmer (again) – Rebus claiming he has an H R Giger on the wall, i.e. this cover
Lester Young – Rebus wonders whether DI Les Young is a Lester like the jazz musician
Mad World – playing in a café (we're guessing Gary Jules' version)

Pub quiz question related
Yellow - Coldplay
Yellow Submarine - The Beatles

Review:

It's hard not to like *Fleshmarket Close*. It's near to the perfect Rebus, with a proper murder to be investigated and a nice fat conspiracy to uncover. Yes, the coincidences come thick and fast and any kind of Rebus romance is ever more unlikely, but given the political situation in the UK at the time of writing (2015) this is the most poignant and relevant of all the Rebus stories for the modern-day reader. It suffers from a lack of focus for Rebus; he's so disenfranchised from the force at this stage that he's almost a commentary on the plot rather than the main man, but it's as near to a conventional story as we'll ever get.

In fact this is nearly an exercise in how to write the perfect crime novel, with all the tropes expected there on the page. Let's list them: the corpse appears on the first page in its opening passage; Rebus arrives at the scene of the murder, the sense of place is established and the scene is set. The first clues start to appear. Rebus is more typically 'gumshoe' here too, with Siobhan playing the younger, more idealistic side-kick. Rebus, the rebel is unwanted by his station, sent to investigate this murder to keep him out the way. His drinking, a cliché perhaps, is actually useful here because he knows all the pubs. He has a sort of failed romance for the sake of having a failed romance and we know the end is nigh: "Over the years, he'd let it push aside everything else: family, friends, pastimes."

The final trope is of course that our hero is just better than everyone else, more brilliant, dedicated, and thorough but this isn't appreciated. As another character notes, he pretends to be "calculating and cynical," but is really something else. It's not that Rebus doesn't care, he just doesn't open up. In a plot that involves people-trafficking and racism, Rebus's own values are clearly decent and liberal, buying toys for the kids at the detention centre, but they are clearly so only to the reader, no-one else gets to know - his moral judgments remain mostly in his thoughts.

By the end the murders have been solved. Convention is satisfied - and contradicted because of the presence of that super criminal Cafferty whose tendrils have touched many aspects of the case is left untouched and above the law.

Highly recommended, and a good one to give to a person starting out with John Rebus…

The Naming of the Dead

Published by: Orion (2006)

Cover: Interior of light streaming through a window, or trees for later editions.

TV adaptation: The penultimate episode, made in 2007. They kept a few of the names and removed the peace conference entirely making a mockery of the title!

One line summary: The G8 comes to town and they try to keep Rebus away from the most powerful people on the planet. Good luck with that.

Four things to notice about The Naming of the Dead:

1. This is the book with the most verisimilitude, with real events that actually happened on the days they happened, with the Rebus/Clarke murder plot woven into the narrative. Recording the G8 shenanigans was part of Rankin's motivation to write this book. He was quoted as saying, "I can think of one cop who won't be involved," and trying to investigate a crime against the back drop. As we'll see Rankin was a little cynical about the whole G8 thing, about whether it would make a difference, and he was right. He even goes to the trouble of getting all the details of the Preston Field House Hotel exactly right for one tiny scene. Even the golf scores are right at the Scottish Open!

2. The Basque separatists line Rebus uses is glorious (one of the best jokes in series) and well done for Rankin acknowledging the source. And it's almost a throwaway. It's so good he uses it twice; he also uses it in a short story

apparently set in a parallel universe (see *The Beat Goes On*).

3. The continuity is better. Rankin notes in various media that the more famous he became the more fans he had who would pick him up on discrepancies. There are clear examples here of Rankin clearing up inconsistencies in the past, although we suspect Rankin doesn't care too much.

4. Rankin is on record about not wanting pat endings to his books, happy to leave things unanswered. But here you have the best punch the air coda in the entire series.

First and Lasts:

It's the first time the dates are really nailed down owing to it happening when the G8 leaders were in Scotland, which saves us a lot of detective work. Rankin even allows some George MacDonald Fraser-esque *Flashman*, or if you prefer *Forrest Gump*-style interference with real events. It transpires that Rebus was responsible for a real accident with George W Bush and a golf buggy.

We have the last appearance (sadly dead) of Rebus's brother Michael, a character who never recovered from the need for him to be a hypnotist in *Knots and Crosses*. It's also the last mention appearance of Bobby Hogan, now a DCI, promoted apparently after the events of *A Question of Blood*, and also the last appearance of Ellen Wylie, a character Rankin never seemed to like.

We also get only the second and therefore the last visits to England in the proper novels, as Rebus gets lost in the way to Coldstream and slips over the border, and then goes south to London.

Background:

We spent a lot of time earlier in the book looking at Rankin's influences. He was very influenced by other writers in his early days but since he became a best-selling author himself he has developed his own style. His inspiration comes from the world around him. He's a news junkie and he knows there are hundreds of issues for him to write about. "The reason I write any novel is that I have questions in my mind about the way the world works," Rankin explained in an interview to promote *The Naming of the Dead.* "I just channel those questions through Rebus and Siobhan." Rankin's novels have become increasingly political, covering immigration, asylum seekers and people-smuggling. "Maybe I am getting more political as I get older," he admitted. "Or maybe these chances are just too good to miss."

When Rankin knew the G8 was coming to Scotland with all the hurly burly associated with it he knew he was going to write about it. He thought about how he felt about the politics and how Rebus wouldn't march, but would watch Pink Floyd at the Live 8 concert, but he also knew Siobhan definitely would march. He knew he had the unique opportunity to get the tone right himself. He attended the marches with his son, he got the vibe down and you feel it in every sentence. But Rankin went further than that. He interviewed staff at the Gleneagles hotel, he chatted to chauffeurs of the VIP's. He spoke to photographers who took pictures at the marches to make sure he had it right. He's proud that he has not been aware of many major howlers. As a full-time writer he was becoming increasingly aware that he had a duty to get his facts right. He also believes that reality makes readers think his books are more believable.

The rest came fairly easily. If you are looking at the G8 the idea of world leaders and capitalists in general, especially the arms trade being criminals in the same way as the more prosaic criminal underworld of Edinburgh street life becomes appealing. Rankin had a few ideas about that too: "A few years ago when I made a series about evil for Channel 4 I interviewed a psychiatrist who said that the psychological make-up of a psychopath is almost identical to that of a successful entrepreneur," he explains. "That is really interesting, that your Murdochs of the world have a pattern of behaviour that is actually quite similar to psychopaths. That has stuck with me and drip-fed its way into a lot of my books."

Rankin assigns a near legendary status to CIRCA, the Clandestine Incendiary Rebel Clown Army, or as he calls them, just the Rebel Clown Army. Art activist John Jordan and colleagues L.M. Bogad, Jen Verson and Matt Trevelyan founded CIRCA in late 2003 to welcome arch-clown George W. Bush on his royal visit to London. CIRCA aimed to be a new methodology of civil disobedience, merging the ancient art of clowning with contemporary tactics of nonviolent direct action. It went on to be a successful meme and international protest phenomenon, with self-organised groups taking action in the streets outside summits and military bases in dozens of countries.

CIRCA worked with professional clowns to develop a methodology, rebel clowning that introduced play and games into the process of political organizing. The Clown army has faded into the memory now of course, like a lot of this. The financial crises of 2008 took attention away from such lofty ideas. But Rankin really did fall for it. He was drawn into it all.

The idea that Rebus was responsible for Bush's bike fall is brilliant and fits what we know about the incident. Officially, according to Scottish police documents, Bush was waving at riot police, but they wouldn't want to admit Rebus was there would they?

The problem with all this accuracy was that Rebus needed to be placed in the plot. There was no way a troublemaker like Rebus was going to be allowed to be part of the policing and Rankin found his answer when he went on holiday after the G8. He went to an area of Scotland north of Inverness called the Black Isle. There he came across a spot called the Clootie Well. From Rankin's webpage: "It's a glade with a small spring emerging from the ground, and local people down the years have left pieces of clothing there for luck – the trees were draped with decaying T-shirts and pants and socks; all very strange. I thought: what a great place for a body! But Black Isle was too remote to make it accessible to Rebus, so I decided to 'move' the Clootie Well to Auchterarder, home of Gleneagles (which just happened to be where the G8 leaders had met). Suddenly, Rebus had a reason for visiting the G8... the story was up and running."

By this stage naming the books often came first but this time Rankin had to work a bit more. When Rankin looked back over his notes, he remembered that some marchers had climbed to the top of Edinburgh's Calton Hill to commemorate the lives lost during the Iraq conflict, in a ceremony they called 'Naming the Dead'. Thanks to them, he now had his title. Rankin not only liked the ceremony name but felt policemen who investigated murders give names to the dead and bring closure for their families. It worked particularly well for the murders in this case.

For those who like to identify the winners of auctions to get their names in the books we have identified a fair few this time. Mollie Clarke won and wanted to be a brothel Madame. As there was no place for one in this story she became a lap dancer. The Colington pharmacy where Rebus buys painkillers also won, as did Steve Dawes and Emma Diprose, who became organisers of the Final Push Glasgow concert in the book.

Things That Don't Make Sense:

Much as there's a big conspiracy going on we still think *someone* would have been there for Ben Webster's autopsy, even if it was just for show.

OK, OK we know by now that coincidence and threads all coming together is a hallmark of the series but how likely is it that

Siobhan finds a piece of missing evidence at the Clootie well near Gleneagles? In addition, in a book where realism is turned up to 11, is it right to create a fictional Clootie well near Gleneagles?

Literally Rankin seems to go all-American at one point when Siobhan is describing the crowd size. He writes: "the local football derby." What's stopping saying Hearts v Hibs? Why the coyness to be Scottish suddenly, especially using 'derby,' a very British phrase for a grudge match?

Another real Rankin observation to question is his description of a steel band as an 'African' steel band: as the instrument used in steel bands is synonymous with Trinidad and Tobago, so we'll have to guess what he actually saw. Other contemporary reports mention African drums, so it's the steel part that is probably wrong.

Not really for this section but does Rankin accept Siobhan's lapsed vegetarian was a slip? He mentions it here.

Did DS Hackman really bring a TV with him? No student would leave theirs in digs, so whose is the TV in the room?

Siobhan's age remains a problem. Rankin now has her visiting Greenham common in the '1980s'. Remember she's a graduate and a DC by 1995, which we felt made her about 25 in 1995 i.e. 35 now, and 15 in 1985 which was the peak of the Greenham Common protests. This makes more sense and is symptomatic of Rankin's new discipline. However, we are going to keep it in this section anyway.

We have the usual vagueness of Rankin with foreign sounding names. Kamwesi sounding more like a Rukigan, west Ugandan name than typically 'Kenyan.'

We get the usual wild coincidences with Santal, although there is a better logic to this one we concede, although how she enters our story is pushing it.

Rebus knows his Shelley after 14 books of being literally ignorant, all fine but he didn't know the name of another Shelley poem 'Yesterday' earlier in the book.

Musical references:

Funeral music
Love Reign o'er me - The Who, leading to Rebus reminiscing about the Who in general: My Generation, Substitute, I Can See for Miles

Rebus's Car music:
Leaders of the Free World - Elbow
Quadrophenia - The Who especially "The real me"

Sundry
Reeling in the Years **-** Steely Dan – reference to their name
Ben Webster **-** the deceased MP shares name with a jazz tenor sax player
Devo video reference someone dressed like them

The Live 8 concert line up
The Who and Pink Floyd, Paul McCartney, U2, Sharleen Spiteri (Texas), Billy Bragg

Rebus's hi-fi
The Groundhogs
Songs of Love and Hate - Leonard Cohen

T-in the park
New Order
The Killers
Keane

Charlie is my Darling - Moira Anderson (music Rebus doesn't want to hear when he's old)

Phrases
Dance with the Devil - Cozy Powell
Money - Pink Floyd ("Don't give me that good-goody-good bullshit" lyric reference)

Lyric reminds him a real life situation
Someone Saved my Life Tonight - Elton John: 'You had me roped and tied' relating to a relationship dynamic
Classic Northern Diversions - Jackie Leven (lyric excerpt - "My boat is so small, and your sea so immense.")

Rebus's Desert Island discs
Would include a song from:
Argus - Wishbone Ash

Clarke's take on the mood in the city
Panic - The Smiths lyric changed to Panic in the streets of Edinburgh

Final Push concert
Texas, Snow Patrol, Corrs (with Bono), Travis, James Brown, Annie Lennox
500 Miles - The Proclaimers
Vienna - Midge Ure
Marti Pellow (Wet Wet Wet)

Sundry
Leaders of the Free World (LP and title track)
Eric Clapton (guess who Brains was named after?)
Clever Trevor - Ian Dury and the Blockheads
Two Against Nature - Steely Dan ("Song lyric?" "Album title.")
Isley Brothers - On hearing of the victims was called Edward Isley
"Does he have a brother?" quips Rebus

Why Does It Always Rain On Me?– Travis – Rebus doesn't like it
Ozzy Osbourne – ozzymandas

Michael Rebus's record collection
Quadrophenia - The Who, Sergeant Pepper - The Beatles, Let it
Bleed - The Rolling Stones, Kinks, Taste, Free, Van der Graaf
Generator, Steve Hillage, Killer - Alice Cooper, Beach Boys,
Hollies, Silver Machine - Hawkwind

Review:

This was widely considered the best of the series at the time; the G8
and the Make Poverty History movement meant a lot to a lot of
people and Rankin's eyewitness interweaving made this seem
cutting edge. A decade on, the classiness and accuracy of Rankin's
observations are less impressive and reviewers like us are sent
rushing to Google to remember who Billy Boyd and Gael Garcia
Bernal actually are/were. It's hard to believe from the perspective of
2005, but even Bono is an irrelevance now. So this has dated badly
and although it seems unbelievable the events here seem as unlikely
as the fictional riot in *Mortal Causes,* which is a shame because it all
really happened. Its predecessor *Fleshmarket Close's* immigration
theme still strikes a chord, this doesn't, and it's a shame because we
bet the events at the time seemed vital. The real shame is that
underneath the reportage is a great Rebus book.

Ironically Rankin gets Mungo the photographer to ask
Rebus whether the protests would make a difference and Rebus says
he lived through the 1968 Paris riots and said it didn't mean
anything at the time, yet it has gone down as important. The irony
being that the G8 protests were the opposite. They meant a lot at the
time but no-one really remembers them now and they had no effect.

Rankin considered it his best novel at the time: *"Black and
Blue* was the breakthrough; that was the first time I felt I knew the
guy and I could do more with the crime novel than just solve a

mystery. Then last year's *The Naming of the Dead* about the 2005 G8 summit; I reread it recently and I thought, 'There's nothing in there I would want to change.' And it got these fantastic reviews, you know – 'Almost transcends the genre' - and sold very well, so I'm truly happy with that book."

The bottom line is it's highly enjoyable but in a frustrating way. It caught the zeitgeist, but the zeitgeist moves on and with ten years' hindsight Rankin over indulged. Is the actual story credible? Looked at dispassionately it's one of the most far-fetched in fact, and one has to question the logic of a story that gets so much pointless detail right but then has to create a Clootie well at Gleneagles.

Exit Music

Published by: Orion 2007

One line summary: It's the end, but it's been prepared for.

Cover: Colourful, moody railings, shot in aquamarine. Later editions were railings without the aquamarine.

TV adaptation: None

Six things to notice about Exit Music:

1) One of the beautiful aspects of Rankin's work is that he never gets jaded and the line in Chapter 16: "Rebus stubbed out his breakfast underfoot," is almost so perfect as to summarise the whole series in six words.

2) "The girls screamed once, only once." Nice opening line, but does it seem a little familiar to you? We won't spoil the joke but let's say there is clear evidence that Rankin reread *Knots and Crosses* before writing this. Did he steal the idea from John Braine, whose *Rabbit Quartet* pulls the same trick, or is it just an obvious idea? If you don't believe us about him re-reading *Knots and Crosses* we offer the following evidence: Rebus's teasing of Siobhan about whether he'd read *Crime and Punishment*, which is probably an in-joke by Rankin at his own folly back when he was starting out. Remember in *Knots and Crosses* it's ludicrously revealed that Rebus rereads *Crime and Punishment* once a year? Also, Rebus even admits to liking jazz again. Oh, and apropos of nothing, a grass called big Podeen turns up...last seen in *Knots and Crosses.* Of course Rebus and Podeen never met in that book but anyways.

3) Are you still playing the game of spot the auctioned names of characters? In the last we'd go for Todd Goodyear, as it doesn't sound like the name of a Scottish PC. Even Rebus queries it, to which PC Goodyear gives a feeble explanation.

4) Because Rankin knew the exact day Rebus was to retire he uses the same verisimilitude style as seen in *The Naming of the Dead*, where he weaves in real events to the fictional ones on the actual days they happened. So we have the right Champions League game happening at the right time etc. But as we'll see this whole book is about real time catching up. If you want a theme then this book's was that Rebus was retiring; there was very little else on anyone's mind and it was all Rankin would be asked to talk about in interviews. Rankin had known for years that Rebus had to retire on a certain date and he was running out of books and Rankin readers have known for several years that some kind of end was coming. So his retirement from the force was always scheduled for November 2006, across 10 days of which *Exit Music* is set. Even this, as Rankin notes is crazy. Most people working in the police get out as soon as they have piled enough years into their pension. But the novels have always made it clear that Rebus remains a policeman because there is nothing else he can bear to be; he has failed as a husband, father, even as a human being - and so *Exit Music* is full of frustrated sadness, Rebus wanting to go no more than the reader wishes him to.

5) This also meant Rankin had to find plenty of ways for him to possibly appear in later books: in interviews he said: he could back in time, stop the clock, or be a cold case researcher, or an unofficial consultant for sure. One thing's for sure he's not going to die.

6)   Rebus reckons 40 bodies over a 30 year career. Sounds about right to us.

Firsts and Lasts:

As it's technically the last book of the Rebus series, there are a lot of lasts, so bear with us if we don't get them all; having said that it's actually not the last Gayfield Square appearance – the post-retirement books are based there. It *is* the last appearances of Phylidda Hawes, Colin Tibbet, James Corbyn, which gives us the last good nickname in 'trouser press'. Also the last appearance of DI Starr, DI Macrae, 'rat arse' Reynolds, Mairie Henderson and DI Starr.

We do get the first appearances of the stalwart modern web pages eBay and Wikipedia.

It took to the end of the original series but we get our first 'god' perspective since *Knots and Crosses* in the first two pages, although even here it's not quite right as 'the man' has a thought at the end.

First product placement, as the girl in the book shop is reading *Labyrinth* by Kate Mosse, a top seller in 2006 - for Orion.

Very, very last hi-fi reference, with Rebus being knowledgeable about cassette tape oxidation, and, as this is like a valedictory book, Rankin even gives us Rebus telling us: "I used to have a thing for hi-fi."

It's last time Rebus gets suspended for no reason but we get a fab scene to reveal it.

Background:

As we've noted before this book is all about kisses to the past, from the first line to the last. Quite how deliberate this was is up for debate. We've alluded to the fact that Rankin knew way beforehand that this would be the last book in the series because Rebus had to retire in 2006, so his thoughts would have always been pushing towards that. This explains the clearly re-read *Knots and Crosses* in preparation, which gives us the sort of obscure detail only a re-read would provide.

It's not named after the Radiohead song *Exit music (from a film)* from *OK Computer* either, but *Exit Music* the debut album (2004) from a fellow Scot Steven Lindsay, who used to front a band called The Big Dish. "It seemed an appropriate title," said Rankin, "Rebus is making his exit, and it's the lead up to the Scottish election in the book, and Scotland could be making its exit from the UK, so as soon as I saw the title I thought: I'll have that. I asked Steven Lindsay if I could use it and he said that was fine. If I had been turned down it would have been called *Inspector Rebus and the Deathly Hallows*.

Actually there's quite a few allusions with Harry Potter in interviews at the time. J.K Rowling had just published her last Harry Potter book to huge media interest and Rankin was a near neighbour. Look at this quote Rankin gave when asked about how hard he found writing the last chapter. Very hard; for once, he did a dozen or more drafts. "I felt even at the end that there was a wee bit of unfinished business. I wasn't staring into space. J.K Rowling said she cried for a couple of days when she finished Harry Potter, but I just went to the pub; that's what Rebus would have wanted."

The book was easy to write. He started it on 1st February 2007 and finished the first draft on 27th March - just two months to write a bestseller. His first draft was rough and had messages like: 'I'M WONDERING IF THE GIRL COULD PLAY A PART IN THE BOOK.' This is the Nancy Sievewright who finds the body right at the beginning of the novel and ends up playing quite an important part in the plot.

As the book is in real time it gives Rankin the chance to use real obituaries to give this a terminal feel: Ferenc Puskas, Jack Palance, Alexander Litvinenko all get a mention, the latter was a particularly fortunate piece of serendipity for Rankin if not for Litvinenko.

The green folder also provided the stereotypes of expensive bills in restaurants, the 2002 incident is the most famous. Five investment bankers spent more than £44,000 on wine at a top London restaurant (Petrus) to celebrate a successful deal. It was reported at the time that the bankers bought a bottle of 1982 Montrachet, for £1,400, followed by three bottles of Chateau Petrus Pomerol - a 1945 vintage costing £11,600, a 1946 at £9,400 and a 1947 at £12,300. Champagne, fruit juice, water and two beers cost a mere £102. Impressed by the choice of wine, the one star Michelins restaurant let the men have their food for free, a £400 saving.

Banking opulence and the finance industry were at their peak at the time. The Celtic tiger economies based on financial industries, all horribly discredited now, were big news, but the SNP at the time were moving towards Scotland thinking about being an independent country, were very keen on promoting the model. The SNP rarely talks about the Celtic Tiger anymore. *Exit Music* and Rankin's next book *Doors Open* really highlight how banks appeared to be these benevolent institutions, with art collections etc. Two years later – big crash and it's as if Rankin knew all along

The political situation in Scotland had been undergoing a renaissance over the previous few years. Scotland, almost totally Labour supporting at the time of devolution had slowly been reassimilating the Scottish National Party into the political system. At the time the SNP was ruling as a minority government. By 2015 their dominance was complete. The case for independence from the rest of the UK was building momentum and it was much talked about. We have to ask is Megan McFarlane based on the then Deputy First Minister Nicola Sturgeon? Rankin was less interested in independence at the time, feeling that he didn't need to be out of the UK to feel more Scottish, but he was curious as to what an independent Scotland would be like. The idea of Russian businessmen tied in with the Russian revolution and the potential revolution in Scotland. He uses Cafferty to make predictions about Scottish independence post-election, who is the sort of person who would profit hugely from such change. "This book was kind of about where Scotland might go in the future," Rankin said. "If it goes independent, does a small country heading for independence attract the wrong kind of folk?

The ban on smoking in public places, which began north of the border ahead of England, is included. The consequent need for Rebus to keep leaving pubs and restaurants ("I'm just going for a tutorial with Professor Nicotine") allows him to see at least one crucial detail out on the streets.

Lastly Rankin's continued art interest comes to the fore again interweaving cool contemporary Scottish artists in with his own creation Roddy Denham.

Oh, and of course you knew that Alba is the Scottish Gaelic name for Scotland so albannach means Scottish. First Albannach bank makes more sense now.

Things That Don't Make Sense:

So, over the space of 17 books we go from the Dostoyevsky reading man of *Knots and Crosses* to the self-confessed unread man who can't even finish Sherlock Holmes' second most famous quote.

Bitchy one this, but Rankin gets a football fact right, with the right score and the right team on the right day. That doesn't make sense!

DC Rat Arse Reynold's first name has changed from Charlie to Ray in the space of two books.

Rebus mentions a case 10-12 years back faking death? Probably Eddie Ringan in *The Black Book*, but this was in 1993 – 14 years ago.

"Five was enough for Enid Blyton" says Siobhan when Rebus notes they have a small team for a murder enquiry, when of course one of the Famous Five was a dog. This is fine until Rankin over does it and adds Goodyear's comment that five worked for Scooby Doo too, and has Siobhan correct him with the line "only if you include the dog." Aaaah!!

Rebus on his one-man stake out of Cafferty and Andropov pretends to check messages on his phone as he stands by a petrol pump. He would be unlikely to get away with this, as it's a major fire hazard.

Rebus makes a joke about the bamboo poles on the side of the Parliament building. They are actually made of oak, but it has gone down in folklore that they are bamboo. It was even reported in *The Scotsman* that work had to be halted on an extension because the submitted plans included bamboo.

Musical references:

CDs in car park office
Kaiser Chiefs, Razorlight, Killers, Strokes, White Stripes, Primal Scream

Music in the Sievewright flat sounded a bit like…
Tangerine Dream

Eddie Gentry related
Bobbie Gentry
Caravan, Fairport Convention, Davey Graham, Pentangle (LPs in Eddie Gentry's flat)

Gifts
Elbow: Leaders of the free world

Sundry
The Gift - Velvet Underground ('White Light/White Heat' LP)

Rebus muses

On poets and their libido:

Don't Go Home With Your Hard-on, True Love Leaves No Traces -
Leonard Cohen ('Death of a Ladies Man' LP)
John Martyn ("One of the great break-up albums..." says Rebus)
Some People Are Crazy, Johnny Too Bad ("...singing my whole life
story.")
Cities - Talking Heads (lyric reference to London being a small city,
so what about Edinburgh?

In Rebus's car

Endless Wire - The Who
Eddie Gentry
Tom Waits (Unspecified LP)

Rebus's leaving present iPod loaded with
"The Stones, Wishbone Ash, you name it..." (what Siobhan has
loaded onto Rebus's iPod)
"John Martyn, Jackie Leven?" (Rebus names his faves)
"...Even a bit of Hawkwind." (Siobhan nails it)

Rebus's hi-fi
Lift Up Every Stone - John Hiatt (from 'Crossing Muddy Waters'
LP)
Jolly Coppers on Parade, You Can't Fool the Fat Man - Randy
Newman ('Little Criminals' LP)
King Crimson
Pete Hamill Rory Gallagher, Page Plant, Jackie Leven, but not
Leonard Cohen

Live at San Quentin - Johnny Cash

Review:

A cozy story the reads like a greatest hits with a rather prosaic ending that is a bit of a damp squib after all the shenanigans before it. This is then followed by a coda that really hits - a classic Rankin ambiguous ending, with Rebus in anguish. The start is almost light hearted especially when compared to some of the mid-period ones.

Fans hoping for a bunch of loose ends to be tied up at the end of the 17th Rebus novel in twenty years are in for a disappointment, not least in the Jekyll and Hyde relationship between Rebus and Cafferty, which is left dangling on the very last page. So this packs an emotional punch but it's because you can feel that Rebus is running out of time and he doesn't want to go, and we don't want him to go either. It has to be read, but it's no classic.

The Non-Rebus books set in Edinburgh

Doors Open (2008)

Doors Open takes the non-Rebus short story, *Herbert in Motion* (from *Beggar's Banquet*) and runs with it. Rankin welding an Ealing comedy style heist caper onto his typically gritty Edinburgh canvas. It's a shame then that for the TV Movie Stephen Fry was perfectly cast as art lecturer Gissing, because that dominates your thoughts in a way that rarely happens with Rankin's work. Sales figures are hard to come by but Rankin claims that ironically this is by far his best-selling book. In truth it's nice enough, and the art theme was almost inevitable but it's Rankin-lite rather than in-depth and you feel that with his clout he could have got away with a much deeper work if he had wanted to at this stage of his career. It's like a Rebus short story and you get the feeling that if Rebus had been in the book he would have spotted the solution way quicker than the police here. You can imagine Rankin's mind working through scenarios, as he got himself a ticket to the real Doors Open event at the National Gallery warehouse.

Perhaps the real question is whether it's set in Rebus's universe or not. We have no problem with it being in a different universe; Gayfield police station is mentioned, although none of the characters we know are mentioned, and a different DI is introduced. No problem until we get a brief allusion to Rebus when Hendricks, the DI says Gayfield station is 'a lot quieter now a certain person has retired'. This causes problems of course, but we can let it slide.

Monboddo is fictional artist, although Rankin collaborated with artist Max Schindler to recreate the Monboddo painting in the book for a competition. The general consensus was that it didn't look like how most people imagined Laura. The rest of the artists mentioned are real.

The Complaints (2009)

The next two books are not John Rebus books per se, but sort of exist in his universe; well we know that now, although at the time of publishing it wasn't so clear. Later, because the main character becomes a major character in the Rebus books, we know they are but there had to be some tweaks to make it happen. With either scenario the books require our attention. The character that is introduced is Inspector Malcolm Fox, a member of The Complaints, the people who investigate police officers. In this case Fox finds he's framed in the murder of his brother-in-law and the story shows us how this straight-down-the-line cop, who is detested by other cops, starts to unravel, as he has to go it alone to find the real killer.

The first thing to say is that Fox feels like a fictional character, an anti-Rebus; his world feels fictional. Is his house real? Is his office real? Is his father's home real? We don't feel the reality. Fox doesn't drink either, a trait that obviously tempted Rankin after Rebus but that makes Fox really frustrating, because it feels such an obvious post-Rebus character trait. And because Fox doesn't drink Rankin has to work hard getting him out there on the streets to follow clues.

Aside from that we have the usual 'real' Edinburgh used as a backdrop. The Tea Tree tea shop existed, but is now closed; Kitchin, a top restaurant is also real. Torpichen police station is also mentioned, although there's no mention of Shug Davidson from Rebus's Torpichen.

What's surprising reading this recently was that we don't feel the bristling resentment that Fox should cause and causes everyone he meets. He's a nasty piece of work and Rankin skillfully works it so we don't hate Fox, and we should, we really should.

There's nothing wrong with the book; we have a frustratingly interesting plot that Rebus could have worked too, with a tweak. The story is actually rather good, fitting in the bank

173

collapse of 2008, stealing Robert Maxwell's fate and delivering a coincidence free plot that's enjoyable. Admittedly it could have been set anywhere, but regular Rebus fans were probably irritated because *The Complaints* is clearly *not* set in Rebus' universe. RBS is a big bank here, not First Albannach, there's even a different Chief Constable.

Despite the rather vanilla lead character, Fox goes about the case the same way Rebus would and even gets suspended. So is it a progression? We mean Fox is a reviled complaints-working, non-drinking, wife beating arse, but that doesn't make him interesting and it's hard to see past Fox being the Ja Ja Binks of the Rebus world.

It's like a Mick Jagger solo album.

The Impossible Dead (2011)

The Impossible Dead has a lot more Complaints work in it, although Rankin sews the seeds for changing the books by noting that in a year Fox will be back in CID. Fox is still a poor man, he hasn't heard of Jimmy Nicholl!

Again the Voodoo room is real, even the pancake place in Kirkcaldy is real

And we get a very Rebusy "scouts' honour" salute, so the typical Rankin style is in place. Rankin even gets the chance to hit the archives. Rankin clearly enjoyed himself, reminiscing through the newspapers of April 1985 like he did for *Black and Blue*. Once again he brings back that era beautifully.

The thing is *The Complaints* was an attempt to write a different kind of police story, which isn't really very good, but *The Impossible Dead* is really good, Rankin writing the type of book he's good at. He just doesn't really want to be writing about the Complaints. It even has an *Edge of Darkness/Scooby Doo* ending – according to the Guardian Reviews.

The only problem with *The Impossible Dead* is that character of Vernal isn't really a fictional character but Scottish nationalist Willie Macrae under not so heavy disguise. Macrae's death details, even down to the make and the colour of the car are correct, which is close to the poor taste of when Rankin narrated using Bible John in *Black and Blue*. He did change the date to the more memorable world snooker final (for British readers) and moved the site of the crash to Fife but everything else is identical. Here, he weaves Macrae's story in with other real names like the Dark Harvest commando. It's a little iffy.

And, as ever the denouement, although exciting is perhaps a little too pat. It involves some very powerful figures getting into trouble because of Fox's off-piste investigation and The Complaints barely coming in to it. Nevertheless it's a cracking Rankin, and the series could have continued with Malcolm Fox who, although detested, *was* carving a niche for himself as a quietly determined police officer.

Then towards the end we realise we are actually in the Rebus universe when a forensics girl remembers a DI who used to describe uniformed officers as woolly suits…

Standing in Another Man's Grave

Published by: Orion (2012)

One line summary: Rebus is back and learning to love the A9.

Cover: Orange day glo cover with the words 'Rebus is Back' written on it. There's a case for the picture on the cover being like the picture in the book: it's remote scenery anyway.

TV series: None

Five things to notice about Standing in Another Man's Grave:

1) As the book cover said: Rebus is back, but it wasn't necessarily the plan, and at the same time he effectively destroys, or certainly rewrites Malcolm Fox. There are a lot of very good reasons not to include Fox in this book, but we'll go into those in the Background section later.

2) The title is a mondegreen, or a mishearing of something. American writer Sylvia Wright coined the term in her essay "The Death of Lady Mondegreen", published in Harper's Magazine in November 1954. The term was inspired by "...and Lady Mondegreen," a misinterpretation of the line "...and laid him on the green," from the Scottish ballad *The Bonnie Earl of Moray*. In this case Rankin himself had misheard the Jackie Leven lyric 'standing in another man's rain'. He just transfers it to Rebus. There are many famous mondegreens: The Beatles 'I can't hide'/'I get high' from *I wanna hold your Hand*, which Bob Dylan takes credit for; 'Scuse me while I kiss this guy' from Jimi Hendrix's *Purple Haze*; 'there's a bathroom on the right' from *Bad Moon Rising*. The English band Prefab Sprout were named after one: Peppered sprout from a Nancy Sinatra lyric. Also, one for old UK readers, the classic Maxell cassette

tape advert using the Desmond Decker song the Israelites: 'my ears are alight.'

3) Miranda Harvey (Rankin's wife) gave an interview to promote this book. She said: "Writing is a very solitary thing to do. You do it yourself in isolation and I suppose Ian really goes into himself. And that can be a bit annoying until I think ah-hah, it is the build up to a novel. Once I realise that's what's happening it's fine because I just sort of get on with life and he's like a teenage student." She also said that she regularly has to reassure him once he has written his first 65 pages and has "run out of steam". She said: "This is I think where it's at its toughest, when he's writing daily, not absolutely certain where he's going. One of my things to do is to remind him of which phase he's in when he's writing. We always talk about the 65 page pause, where he has poured on to the page all of the things he's thought about and rehearsed, all of his ideas are down in black and white and then he kind of runs out of steam and he'll always say, 'it's going really badly,' and I'll say, 'oh yes, page 65' and he says, 'I am at page 65', and I say, 'it'll be all right'. And he also panics around two thirds of the way through, when he still doesn't know what will happen in the book."

4) Sometimes the process writing this book was joyous and brought a smile to the face when we unearthed a good fact. A good example was when Rebus takes a book he borrowed from the hotel library up to his room. Now this was a very un-Rebusy thing to do, so we googled the title, *Cracking the Code*, assuming it would be the Paul Azinger golf book. The result that intrigued us was the one with the subtitle *Cracking the Code: Understand and Profit from the Biotech Revolution That Will Transform Our Lives and Generate Fortunes* by one Jim Mellon. Why did it intrigue us? Well Jim Mellon was also the name of the farmer

nearer Edderton in the book. And we have found another winner of a 'get your name in an Ian Rankin book' auction! Jim Mellon actually has four times more followers on Twitter than Ian Rankin and according to one interview he is Britain's answer to Warren Buffett. His mother was from Edinburgh and he was born there and is a regular in *The Sunday Times* rich list.

5) Ian Rankin is a one-finger typist.

Firsts and Lasts:

DI James Page and DC Esson make their debuts as a sort of modern take on policing; it's also the first time Siobhan is a Detective Inspector. James Page is sort of inferred as a bit of a squeeze for Siobhan, which is nearly a first, but see 'Things that Don't Make Sense'. First book with a little by-line on the front, in this case 'Rebus is back.' First time we see Siobhan as a DI and Rebus not really a police officer. First mention of Malcolm Fox and his team, but this is a stiffer Malcolm Fox than the almost rebellious Fox of the last book. Perhaps he just really hates Rebus? First book for a long time with no quotations at the beginning. First time we know what brand of cigarettes Rebus prefers: Silk Cut. First use of a map to help us get a grip of things (certainly in the hardback). First book in a while not to mention Rankin was 'born in the Kingdom of Fife'.

Background:

As we know Rankin writes one book every year and as 2011 drew to a close he knew it was time to start the next one. Luckily for us he kept a video diary during the writing process for the BBC documentary *Imagine...Ian Rankin and the Case of the Disappearing Detective*. The Rankin green folder of ideas had mention of a missing girl on the A9 and this got Rankin thinking this time around. Further research brought up the case of Renee

MacRae, who disappeared on the A9 in 1976. This was officially the UK's longest running missing person case and was still getting periodical coverage in the Scottish press. Also Claudia Lawrence, an English chef who disappeared in 2009 was still fresh and relevant, and even as we write arrests are being made. Rankin comments in the documentary about a man going up and down the A9 looking for his daughter, but this is harder to trace. The documentary allows us to have almost day-by-day knowledge of the writing process.

So January 2nd was spent procrastinating and writing up his notes. It was raining. On January 8th he got a haircut and planned to start writing 'tomorrow'. 'Tomorrow' saw him sitting in Starbucks, reading the newspaper, pretending it was research. Later that day he put the Tangerine Dream album on, his writing music, this triggered the process and the first lines were written. He'd just been to a funeral and he wrote about that. In the documentary, shown way before the book came out we listened to the opening words read out and when the words, 'Christ he needed a cigarette' were uttered it was bloody obvious that REBUS WAS BACK. There were tears in our eyes and we leapt around the room. Rankin swore he didn't know he was going to bring Rebus back, but as he wrote those words he knew it was Rebus and that John Rebus, working on cold cases would be the best person to look into the missing girls. It would have been very difficult to shoehorn Malcolm Fox of the Complaints into this storyline. It should be stated that we the reader don't know for sure he had been working in cold cases; in *Exit Music* he was considering applying, but the only way we know is because Rankin kept telling us during interviews. While we're on the subject, the wooden suit line about a coffin is lovely.

Rankin was bugged by the Rebus return. Could he justify it? He knew Rebus's return would be big news and prepared himself for the inevitable conclusion that Malcolm Fox had failed as a lead character. Once Rankin decided that he was bringing Rebus back he decided he could contrast modern policing to Rebus. This allows us to be introduced to a whole new range of policemen, including the now ubiquitous 21st Century geek in hot water-drinking DC Christine Esson.

January 30th: 2012 Rankin, looking rough, tells the camera he had got 'the fear'. As noted above Miranda knows it'll be because he has reached page 65 and this always happens, but Rankin lets us see the note above his computer, which is a quote from Iris Murdoch: 'every book is the wreck of a good idea.' So he was in a positive frame of mind.

By 16th February he still had the fear but was writing 'good stuff' that pushed the plot forward. On 5th March the first draft was done, it was ragged, but he'd seen worse first drafts. He had got to within nine pages of the end without knowing who did it, a record, he says, although this contradicts other quotes by him.

During the writing of the first draft Rankin had made the decision to bring in Malcolm Fox, essentially looking into Rebus because Rebus was re-applying to join CID. The first thing to notice is that this is a different Fox. Even though Rankin swears he's a nice guy in his own books in this Rebus book he's 'a shit'. This was inevitable seeing him through Rebus's eyes, but the logic of doing this worried Rankin.

16th April: Rankin goes on a fact checking drive up the A9, checking the mileage, checking out the Inverness police station with his own eyes. He also checked Rosemarkie for a major scene. He was also delighted that Edderton was exactly as he imagined it. The glorious line in the book where Rebus feels he's 'never been further away from a pub' is thought up by Rankin on this journey for the cameras and it's so good he jokes he'll use it.

"Rebus is back" was the big announcement at the Hay-on-Wye book festival that summer. It went down very well and the press response was huge, but Rankin was affronted by an article by Tiffany Jennings in *The Scotsman* entitled: "Rebus is returning and he's in good company." Jennings asserted that the comeback was unoriginal and too convenient. She analogized it to rock stars making comebacks, and to society's addiction to the past. In truth this stinks of a classic newspaper brainstormed opinion piece, but as we know Rankin is very sensitive. The article ended with the line: "Rebus mate, you're past it. Stop embarrassing yourself." Rankin mused on it for a while and said, "Only if it's a crap book is it not worth bringing him back."

11th June: the third draft went to Caroline Oakley his editor. She enjoyed it but wanted the prologue tighter and questioned the inclusion of Malcolm Fox. We all question the inclusion of Malcolm Fox! Rebus takes the criticism badly, as ever and questioned how he still can't get this writing thing right after 25 years.

28th June, at nearly 1 a.m. the book was finished. Rankin was bored with it and wanted to move to the next project.

Musical References:

Title and Prologue
As we know Standing in Another Man's Grave is a misheard lyric from a Jackie Leven song 'Standing in Another Man's Rain' ("Time to get your ears checked, muttered Rebus to himself")

Dedication
RIP Jackie Leven

Hi-fi music
Unspecified Rory Gallagher album
Astral Weeks - Van Morrison

The start of a running joke by Rebus on the name of Siobhan's new boss, DCI James Page

So we get various Led Zeppelin song: Mr. 'Dazed and Confused', Physical Graffiti, Communication Breakdown, Custard Pie, Trampled Underfoot - this time from DC Esson.

In Siobhan's Audi on the first trip up the A9

Rebus replaces Kate Bush's *Fifty Words for Snow* with Jackie Leven then puts Kate back on again ('She seemed to be singing about her love for a snowman'). This is probably Misty released late November 2011.

Mix tape for road music
Canned Heat, Rolling Stones, Manfred Mann, Doors (theoretical mix tape for songs about roads)

I Still haven't found what I'm looking for – Rebus uses is to use a song to express a life

Maggie Bell (playing on the radio - he wondered if she was still going strong)

Rebus's hi-fi
After Bert Jansch it was the turn of the Stones, and after that some Gerry Rafferty
Nazareth
Rebus replaces John Martyn with some early Wishbone Ash.

Things That Don't Make Sense:

Rebus is 64 years old, possibly 65, yet here he's smoking and drinking, keeping long hours and getting into a very intense fight with a villain, and other escapades. He should be dead of heart failure after all this. We think Rankin may have forgotten how old he is. Part of the problem is that Rankin has always felt Rebus in his gut and ages him to his own age. It's a problem here, although we think Rebus is rather heroic.

Cracking the Code: Understand and Profit from the Biotech Revolution That Will Transform Our Lives and Generate Fortunes is a hugely unlikely book to be in a hotel reception library.

Rebus tells Siobhan about a case before she joined CID where he nearly lost Sammy: Like they've never spoken about *that* before in 20 years.

These are the ones we love: when Rebus is waiting for Susie Mercer he 'plucked a nacho from the bag and popped it in his mouth'. He means a tortilla chip. Nachos is a dish with tortilla chips (totopos) covered in cheese salsa and other goodness.

Fox never mentioned Rebus in 'his' books although one character alludes to him; here Fox knew him at St Leonard's and always hated him. We never met Fox before and he was never mentioned in the St Leonard's-set books. Rankin is rewriting history.

Malcolm Fox is portrayed as a man who recycles and doesn't take files home with him. Yet the Malcolm Fox in *The Complaints does* take files home.

The grainy photograph of countryside that holds the plot together does not like the photo on the book cover. And while we're at it the map in hardback isn't the most useful ever put in a book.

Bit desperate this but Siobhan went to the hydroelectric dam in the book as a kid - but she lived in England then. Would she really?

We're not sure if this should be in this section but a DC Ormiston gets a brief mention in this book. Old hands like us assume this is Ormie from earlier books going back to *Mortal Causes*, but it's not him. This one is called Dave, the previous one never got a first name and he's far too young. We're just wondering Why Ian!?

Review:

From the opening chapter which feels like a short story or a reintroduction, Rankin does a very good job of not letting us settle down to another cozy Rebus tale. There is a feeling of uselessness ringing through in a way we've not had before This is an older Rebus, one who knows his time is up and he's working essentially to stop himself drinking himself to death. His friends are dying and his style of policing is considered about as relevant as dinosaur biology. Snitches are gone, the internet and search engines and social media work just as well, if not better than the old ways. He knows he's finished, but feels, like we all do in such situations that our way was the right way, the pure way and that we're BETTER somehow. So this is unsettling because we root for him and he does a lot of the work and gut feeling intuition here despite all the sophistication of the methods employed elsewhere, and he gets very little thanks for it on the surface.

The beauty of this book is that on first reading you're just pleased he's back, on second reading you note how sad it all is. Rebus hasn't moved on but the world has. This book is well-crafted, melancholic, with a nice right plot and some proper sleuthing, less coincidency than Rankin usually gives us and the paradoxical truth that Rebus sometimes is better outside Edinburgh is never more true. The new cast are bland, which could be a clever ironic statement from Rankin, or maybe not. The ending however is a little flat. We wrote about how Rankin didn't know who the killer was until the end and it feels like it; we never understand the motivation, and Rankin leaves us in the dark with the ending too. In the documentary Rankin joked about including a clichéd 'killer's point of view opening scene' as the knife flashes down but decided against it: the privilege of the million seller, and it is quite a cliché, but ironically there's quite a good case for one here, because we just don't *get* the killer. But of course this isn't about the killer, it's about the themes: loss, memory, mortality and letting go.

The beauty of the scene in Tongue where unannounced and unfussily Rebus knocks on his daughter's door but without answer: it broke our hearts.

That's the genius of Rebus; he gets older, so he never gets tired as a character. He's not preserved like Poirot. So in retirement every third thought is his grave. Even surveying his collection of old concert tickets brings on intimations of mortality: "just one more thing to be binned when he was no longer around." Some of the most moving passages in the book are his reflections on the musicians of his own age - Jackie Leven, John Martyn, Bert Jansch - who have died since we last encountered him.

On the downside Malcolm Fox doesn't work and was nearly a spectacular own goal. The section on Fox p191-192 of the UK hardback does for him. He is written as the absolute antithesis of Rebus. This is a meaner spirited Fox yet that universe of his books and this universe are not quite linked. Was that a fictional heroic Fox and this the real one?

In the end just be thankful Rebus is back, and the end line is the best in the whole series.

Saints of the Shadow Bible

Published by: Orion (2013)

One-line summary: Rebus is back in the force as a DS investigating some old colleagues before the Complaints can get them.

Cover: Bright yellow day glo cover of stratocumulus clouds taken from the centre of an ornate Edinburgh street. It has the words: Rebus – Saint or Sinner? on the front.

Five things to notice about Saints of the Shadow Bible:

1) It's hard to avoid the influence of the TV Series *Life on Mars* here. The cliché of corrupt cops from the past had become a trope of the early 21st Century and Rankin gives us his take on the concept here, with some characters who make Gene Hunt look soft.

2) First mention of the Waterboys song playing in Fox's car. They are the one Scottish band Rankin never mentions in the books until now, yet he's publically called singer Mike Scott a genius, loved their W B Yeats inspired album and their biggest hit *The Whole of the Moon* was on his playlist for the Guardian. The two are pals and made friends via Twitter. Rankin even introduced Mike Scott at Scott's autobiography launch in 2012, which was when this book was being written.

3) The fact that Rebus is in CID is remarkable given his age. Rankin got the idea from a fan at a forum who said that fans should start petitioning the Scottish parliament to change the age of retirement for cops so that Rebus can stick around until he's 65. Rankin has mentioned that the Minister responsible was a fan, although there's no evidence this is true.

4) Not really relevant to *Saints,* but it crossed our minds while reading it: we never get a colour for the Saab. Rankin has pointed this out in another tweet. The consensus is usually that it was dark grey, or silver. We can't argue with that.

5) We liked the sartorial reference to brown shoes where Rebus bitches to Fox about his brown shoes. He makes a reference to the Frank Zappa song *Brown Shoes Don't Make It* when Fox has committed that particular faux pas. Fox has never heard of Zappa, and Rebus makes a big deal of this and the fact that Fox 'hardly ever listens to music.' Sartorially of course Rebus and Zappa are slightly wrong. The etiquette books tell us brown shoes *are* acceptable with blue jeans and if you're hip and trendy then you can get away with it with blue suits too, otherwise brown shoes and tweed are just vital. Just for the record men, NEVER wear black shoes with jeans.

First and Lasts:

At last, after nearly twenty books Rankin finally tells us exactly where Rebus lives: 17 Arden Street. This caused press attention on its own. The Daily Record printed pictures, including the living room. We've included the link in the afterword.

Clutching at straws, but this is the last book where we get any description of Rebus. Here he is described as overweight, with a girth similar to that of a bouncer who goes to the gym regularly. So Rebus has definitely let himself go (surprise surprise) but we wonder whether despite his protestations Rankin has been a little influenced by knowing Ken Stott played Rebus...

We have our last Stones reference, but this is also the first time since the first book that Rebus is in the police but not a DI. We also get our first music segue since the late 1990s.

Last mention of Prof Gates, who seems to have died sometime after 2007, nice to tell us Ian. Last Jackie Leven title too, but the first mention of the now ubiquitous iPad and Google.

Background:

Rankin said it started with a retirement party he attended, with lots of old cops telling outrageous stories about the way that policing used to be in the early 1980s. The stories were so good Rankin would excuse himself and go away and type all the stories into his phone. It got him thinking, when we first met Rebus he'd already been a detective for several years – so how did he become the cop that he became? On top of that the police in Scotland were doing away with double jeopardy, which meant they could prosecute old crimes even if a person had been found not guilty, so he wanted to include that as well. He also had to deal with the restructuring of Scotland's police. 2013 saw the start of Police Scotland replacing all the previous divisions. Rankin goes with it and even the new Chief Constable in this book is from the same force (Strathclyde) as in the real world.

Gene Hunt's influence is huge here in that Rebus and his old cronies represents that kind of dinosaur, that sort of old-style cop with a bottle of whisky in the bottom drawer who would give the suspect a slap in the interview room. That type of policing is pretty much gone now but Rankin liked the idea of comparing that to the new style policing and of course to Mr. Straight Edge, Malcolm Fox. The investigation into the Saints allows Fox to come into the story legitimately but also allows Rebus and him to work together to remove all the mutual loathing.

"Most of the cops Rebus works with think his way of doing things just doesn't work anymore," said Rankin. "The world is changing very quickly and in the last couple of books mortality's kind of staring him in the face. But in this new book he proves himself useful in various ways. I mean none of these young, nice touchy-feely cops have got grasses they can go and talk to in seedy pubs around the city, they're too busy sitting at their computers or on Twitter or Facebook."

Despite Rankin's perhaps reluctance to discuss the 2015 referendum it looms over so much here and Rankin had to write about the build-up. "When you have conflict, when you have times being uncertain, when you have political instability it makes for very interesting books. Rebus is a conservative with a small c, he doesn't like change, he doesn't trust change, he is very much someone who enjoys the status quo and for that reason, if no other, he'd probably vote no." But in an interview Rankin gave to a Surrey newspaper he said he felt English Siobhan would vote yes. The author, a proud Scot said he had his doubts about the SNP's plans for independence and has said he was somewhere in the middle. He said: "Independence can't make me feel any more Scottish than I already feel."

As we'll see for the next entry someone involved with producing this book was reluctant to write about the 2015 Referendum. Orion, Rankin insisted, told him to remove a reference to the First Minister's special advisor, a character who was in the book even in quite a late draft. Rankin has also suggested that Orion would have preferred to avoid the emotive issue of independence completely.

"There was a character in the new book who was a special adviser to the First Minister. But my publisher felt it slowed things down too much, this political sub-text, so she went. Because she is no longer in the book, there is no longer a connection to the First Minister's office. But I did like my special adviser - I am going to have to try to bring her back in some guise."

Musical References:

Sundry

Siobhan references pioneering Aussie punk band The Saints. Fox: 'you maybe won't have heard of the Saints?'. Clarke: 'Only the band.'
'The Saints are coming' - The Skids
Charlie Watts (Rebus compares policing to Charlie's life as a Rolling Stone - 'ten years spent drumming, and the other forty spent waiting for something to happen').
'Is that all there is?' Peggy Lee
BB King (ringtone)
Neil Young Glasgow concert - 13 June 2013 (Rebus wasn't planning to go 'They only had standing')
David Bowie 1983 Murrayfield concert
Duran Duran ('80s night at The Gimlet')

Car Songs

Unspecified Mick Taylor CD
Unspecified Waterboys song

Commenting on the action

Rebus references that Jona Lewie classic 'Always find me in the kitchen at parties'
'Shakier than a Neil Young tribute band'
'Brown Shoes Don't Make It' Frank Zappa

Rebus' hi-fi
Unspecified Miles Davis LP ('from the period before he got weird')
'So What' Miles Davis

Spooky Tooth's second album (Spooky Two)
Hardnose the Highway LP - Van Morrison (Rebus puts on side 2 -
'but he wasn't really listening')
Beggars Banquet LP - The Rolling Stones ('How had he managed to
sleep through so much of that?' - Rebus nods off during Side 2)
Solid Air LP - John Martyn

Things That Don't Make Sense:

Let's get the standing agenda point of Siobhan's age out of the way
quickly. As we've noted, at very best Siobhan is 41, probably 44. Is
she really dating Jimmy Page and now David Galvin, both in their
very early thirties. We're convinced Rankin thinks Siobhan is early
30s, scrub that, we KNOW.

This book pretty much confirms that *Knots and Crosses*
was definitely set in 1987, as Rebus confirms he was shot in1987;
this is a rare event, and Rebus was shot in that book. This book also
claims that soon after he was recently promoted to DI. All fine, but
this doesn't help the early Rebus timeline issues. Remember in *Hide
and Seek*, published in 1991, he seemed to be getting used to his
promotion. Four years to get used to a promotion seems too much!

Talking of timelines and dating we love the Saints'
background, but it's tough to fit it in. We've not heard the slightest
whiff of them before, which is odd to say the least, but here Rebus is
a DC in 1982 and we're told he is a DS by 1987 and a DI soon after.
It's all rather concertinaed in if you ask us, especially as DS's often
do five years. Rankin would have been better off sticking to the
1991 timeline, which fits much better. The other problem is the
Lenny Spaven storyline from *Black and Blue*. There we had Rebus
as a young CID officer involved with another boss perhaps faking
evidence. Perhaps even for Rebus this is too much dodginess in one
backstory for both these events.

Rebus compares policing to Charlie's Watts' life as a
Rolling Stone - 'ten (years) spent drumming, and the other forty

191

spent waiting for something to happen'). The quote is actually, 'work five years, twenty years hanging around.'

Rankin claims Siobhan and Fox had met before 'but just barely,' yet in *Standing in Another Man's Grave* it was claimed that Fox knew Rankin from St Leonard's, and if you knew Rebus back then then you'd know his self-confessed best friend...

Rankin infers that the Ox was a police haunt back in the day (1982) and that Rebus was a regular, but as we know it took him six books to even mention it. This is a good case of Rankin telling the truth, but forgetting his own fiction.

Weirdly and very out of character Rankin gives away the murderer in *Standing in Another Man's Grave* as he reintroduces us to Daryl Christie in one if his pubs.

Maggie, Rebus's near ex-squeeze is repeatedly described as looking radiant – she's 65 years old. We're not saying 65 year old women can't look radiant but it's not the first word that springs to mind. And talking of ages Rebus is back in CID because they raised the retirement age to 65, but he's older than 65.

Finally, Rebus claims he redecorated flat ten years ago. As we know this book is set in spring 2013 (The Neil Young concert) that means 2003, but it was actually in *Black and Blue* in 1986, nearly 20 years ago.

Review:

How does he keep doing it? Rankin produces another cracking page-turner, with a hugely satisfying plot resolution. It has to be said that this feels briefer, less dense, less important somehow. With three lead characters something has to give, and it's Edinburgh as a character having to take a back seat and the range is weaker because of it. A closer reading gives us a very light book. Although the Saints are an interesting diversion (and for once Rankin doesn't merge the cases in the book) it doesn't really go anywhere and we're left with the cliché de jour of old Skool policing, although the lovely prologue and epilogue that bookend the actual story show us Rebus hasn't forgotten all the old tricks in this world of modern nickname-free policing. So we have a flimsy little tale that has some wonderful sleuthing even if it requires two errors by the police for the case to last a whole book. Also, we don't get enough of the Saints, and we struggle to see how dirty Rebus was. Rankin was pleased about that: "I'm glad I didn't give it away too early. I like there to be a bit of moral ambiguity. Right at the end of the book you go, 'Oh, wait a minute – is he really a nasty piece of work?' Although I'm on his side, is he the kind of guy who's best avoided if you were to meet him in real life? The answer to that is 'probably'. I was trying to get across to the reader there are games being played here, and what's being said may not necessarily be what the person really thinks. You're never very sure, are they going to hinder each other or are they going to come to a mutual understanding?"

This is all well and good but anybody reading Rebus for long enough knows Rebus isn't dirty, so it plays a little false and lessens the drama for the long-term reader.

The good thing is that Rankin has pulled off the impossible and Rebus and Fox are grudgingly respectful by the end. This allows Fox to be rehabilitated after the disaster of the previous book and opens the way for more three-pronged tales in the future.

The Beat Goes On

Published by: Orion (2014)

Notes:

In 2013 Rankin revealed he was taking a year off work because of health fears. Publicising the debut of his first stage play *Dark Road* in September 2013. He said "I'm going to have a year off next year. I'm knackered, basically. Bluntly, I'm just shattered. I need the batteries recharging big-time." He said he was shaken by good friends such as Iain Banks and Gavin Wallace, long-time head of literature at the Scottish Arts Council, "dropping dead". He went on: "The kids are on the cusp of leaving home, or have left home. Friends of mine are dropping dead. Gavin Wallace dropped dead at the age of 53 earlier this year. I'm 53. Then of course Iain Banks was taken from us at the age of 59. I don't want to die slumped over my desk. So I'm taking a year off next year and doing some travelling."

We've alluded to this before but taking a year out solved a problem of timing with the Scottish Referendum dominating Scottish life in 2014 any book Rankin wrote would be tainted if he got the referendum result the wrong way round. Rankin hinted that Orion were aware of that. When he was asked if there would be a Rebus novel set against the backdrop of the campaign, he said: "Not if my publisher has anything to do with it."

So this was compiled in the interim, with contractual obligation in mind. The stories are all of the previously compiled short-stories plus, we say flippantly, all the ones Rankin remembered to include, which means there are some gaps.

Below are the stories not discussed before.

Dead and Buried

Written for this collection. In his published work this is the only time Rankin has written a story in about the past and a young Rebus. Here we meet the characters recently created for *Saints of the Shadow Bible*. It's set in 1983, but deals with a far older case. The Saints are up to their usual tricks and Rebus gets to fully appreciate that. It's fluff and doesn't add much to our knowledge and there isn't enough period detail to make it stand-out.

Tell me who to kill (2003)

Slick and confident, with perhaps one too many characters, although this story formally published means we get our first ethnic minorities in Alexis Ojiwa and wife. It's a Kenyan name, not super known for football playing, but there we go. Hard to dislike, very Rebus, almost too Rebus with the bookended Oxford bar but when you realise it was a collection for 50 years of the Crime Writers' Association that shouldn't surprise you.

Saint Nicked (2002)

A couple of excruciating puns, a reaffirmation of Rankin's assertion that writing about music always seems false, a gem of an idea for a heist but peppered with Rankin's typical lighthearted short story style which means you don't take it as seriously as the story deserves. And Jean Burchill never appealed to us and isn't going to now.

Atonement (2005)

This was written for the omnibus edition of *A Good Hanging* and *Beggars Banquet*. We'll repeat this, yes there was an omnibus edition of the short stories, which means it's a bit like *The Beat Goes*

On. How many times can you go to the well Orion? It's hard to dislike, melancholic and poignant. A little picture of a caring John Rebus. A little implausible and a painting involved but you kind of expect that now.

Not just another Saturday (2006)

Set during the Make Poverty History March on 2nd July 2005, which means it happened concurrently with *The Naming of the Dead* and Rebus did none of these things that Saturday. Rankin even recycles his best (stolen) joke from that book – go on, guess. OK, OK this clearly came first, and seeded a lot of the material but it's weird anyway. Nice enough portrait of our man watching the marches and preferring the Ox. This was written just after the event for the SNIP charity (special needs information point).

Penalty Claus (Daily Mail 2010)

The date above is a little false. It may have been published then but it's set between 2004 and 2007, as Rebus takes the anti-heroes to Gayfield. It's a little neat, by this stage Rankin is writing stories to order for Christmas and this is a little too cute and tidy

The Passenger (2013)

Named after the Iggy Pop song and really good. It seems to be written for this collection but dating it is very tricky. Clarke is in charge and the phrase 'bucket list' is used, which is modern to UK ears. This is exactly what short stories are for. Rankin finally pays off his own perceived huge debt by referencing *The Driver's Seat*, Muriel spark's brilliant novel from 1970 that would have won the Booker prize that year had it been awarded (a long story). The plot line is similar and the result just as powerful and remains one of the more disturbingly good stories from the Rebus canon.

Three-pint problem (2013)

With its allusions to Sherlock Holmes in the title from *the Red Headed League*, 3 pipes and 50 minutes to solve the case. This is set in 2014 for sure, as Rebus is DS. Sir Arthur Conan Doyle was supposedly the orchestrator of a cruel joke. One night, bored and idly toying with wicked thoughts, he decided to send a note to five of his friends. The note would be delivered anonymously. It would have no signature, and would contain no information. It would only say, "We are discovered. Flee!"

At his next dinner party, his social circle was abuzz with the sudden, and total, disappearance of one of the people he sent the notes to. The person was never heard from again.

But the story didn't start or end with him. Edgar Allan Poe was also said to have done such a thing. He might even be said to be the better author to pair with the story, since he had more of a devilish sense of humor. Actually, neither man probably did this. The story of the notes is an old joke going back centuries. Supposedly it was used by politicians of one party to get members of the other party to flee before an important vote.

It is just a joke, but there's a reason why it's associated with so many mystery authors and so many tests of virtue. What better than such a note to illuminate the secret lives that some percentage of the population are living. This is one of the few jokes that we would love to see turned into a sociological survey. What percentage of the population, were they to receive such a note, would take the advice? Once you hear the story of course you write a short story! The consequences are that we get probably the best of Rankin's short stories, so good it could fit as a whole novel.

Read out loud in 2008 at the Caledonian brewery in aid of another charity this features the newly retired Rebus on a tour with Siobhan. It's not bad but Rebus is almost superhuman in sniffing out murders here.

Comment:

For reasons outlined above Rankin decided to not release a novel in 2014 and so this was cobbled together to fill the gap. It's a bit of a con, with *A Good Hanging* and *Beggar's Banquet* all back, and they had already been put together ten years earlier. And the archiving of the unpublished stories was a little slack, as the next section will detail.

Other short stories missed by The Beat Goes On

These stories for unknown reasons did not make it into the definitive collection called *The Beat Goes On*. We started worrying when Rankin tweeted that one story was found just after going to press. Well there are more than that. We've given details of five below and we are currently on the trail of a sixth as we go to press. If you can help us source it to read please get in touch (we're on Twitter) or if you'd like help sourcing these stories because you're curious let us know as well.

Well Shot (1995) this appeared in 2nd Culprit, a CWA annual (us) edited by Lisa Cody and Michael Lewin

Featuring DCI Frank Lauderdale and Rebus at a siege. Very early mobile phone reference (called a portable phone). It's a mystery why this story was forgotten about as it's a) very good, b) very different, as it concerns a gun siege and Rebus refusing to be fooled by what he'd seen. Worth tracking down despite the unlikely sophistication of the protagonists.

The Acid Test (1998) Published in *Edit*, the magazine for alumni of Edinburgh University in 1999. Back editions of the magazine are available as PDFs on the alumni web page.

An interesting tale that foreshadows the story he was about to begin, *Set in Darkness* with a body discovered in tunnels under the university. Rebus is our way in but Prof Gates does the research in his spare time. Although the reveal makes you smile it verges on the ridiculous and is written to make graduates smile.

Get Shortie (1999) This appeared in Crimewave 2 'Deepest Red' published by TTA press and coming out of the UK.

Get Shortie is another Christmas tale with no detection apart from Rebus knowing every villain with a heart in the city and it's hardly surprising that Rankin forgot about it. The punchline/title is a play (and a rather forced one) on a Scottish food item and the Elmore Leonard book and the film, which were quite hip at the time., We're guessing it was written in 1995 when the film came out but forgotten about until 1999 when it was given to the publication. Given the huge spread of adverts for Rankin's publisher in this edition, not just for Rankin you do detect the hand of the publicity machine forcing Rankin to find something for the book.

Fieldwork (from Ox-tales Earth - an Oxfam charity collection 2009)

Rankin rarely talks about short stories but when he does he often mentions the concept of the purity of telling a story in the fewest amount of words, occasionally mentioning a 200-word story he wrote as an example. Well, here is that story. Originally written for the famous Hay-on-Wye book festival who wanted some 200 word stories. Apparently the original had 202, but this one is 200 - except it's 199 words, or 204 if you count words like 'it's' as two words, which you should. It's what it is for 200 but let's say we think the victim was taking the piss.

In the Nick of Time (2014)

This appeared in *Face Off*, a David Baldacci edited book of short stories with the tag line 'all your favourite writers, all your favourite characters. It's time for them to Face Off.' Essentially it has two writers with their characters telling one story, which is very squee if you pardon the fannish language. Rankin wrote his with Peter James, horror writer turned police procedural writer who has created Roy Grace a detective based in Brighton. Rankin keeps the really

Rebus' detail to a minimum in deference to readers who will be new to him, but it also gives us Rebus written by someone else for the first time in the scenes written by James. The story itself is stretched so tight to allow the cops to meet it ends up being ludicrous but it's still worth tracking down. It'll make you smile.

Squee!

Even Dogs in the Wild

Published by: Orion 2015

One line summary: Well, if you Google the lyrics of the song from which the title is taken then you'll find what this book is really all about - so don't do it.

Cover: In the style of the previous three Rankin books but in shocking pink, with a black and white picture of a broken wooden cross in a field. See Firsts and Lasts.

Five things to notice about Even Dogs in the Wild:

1) As we've noted already the title is from a song by The Associates, or as one of the characters in the book says more accurately, that bloke who 'sounds like his balls are in a vice'. They were a Scottish band of the early 1980s. They had one huge hit with a song called *Party Fears Too*, which really emphasised singer Billy Mckensie's extraordinary falsetto range. It remains probably the most impossible song ever to try at a karaoke night. Another memory for us is their performance on *Top of the Pops* of *18 Carat Love Affair* where the guitarist was over enthusiastically miming his disco strumming and broke the neck off his guitar causing corpsing all round. This seemed to be the only happy point in the whole career of the band, who lost momentum soon after this due to Mckensie's reluctance to tour. Mckensie's committed suicide in 1997 age 39. *Even Dogs in the Wild* was on the first album called *The Affectionate Punch*, released a couple of years before they hit the big time. See Things That Don't Make Sense.

2) Malcolm Fox is getting a lot of the attention in this book and there's an argument that he's the main character here. If you don't believe us let's look. He's the first character to appear outside the

prologue, his name is the first two words of the book's blurb. The last chapter is set in his world. He's having a thing with Siobhan (don't worry, we're coming to this), he gets bloodied and beaten and most of the sleuthing is done by him. This is his story...get over it.

3) Rankin, whether he knows it or not, has changed his style a bit of late. Not the prose so much, he's interested in verisimilitude as ever, but it manifests itself in different ways. Here he pays great attention to listing every car make, where before he would have little interest (it took him six books to decide Rebus's car was a Saab). He names supermarket chains and even puts a quick scene in the Canongate Starbucks he's been known to 'research' in. It's not for us to criticise such a thing, it's the modern way, but we worry that this might date the books unnecessarily for future readers.

4) We're slightly disappointed that in 2015 when Rankin gives us a family called the Starks and he doesn't make the obvious *Game of Thrones* reference. This is probably because Rankin hasn't read the books, nor seen the series, but a lot of his readers will. Now don't get us wrong, there's no way Rebus will pick up the reference either but we've got a pretty strong feeling that Fox would like a bit of *Thrones* action. He needs to have something to be interested in anyway! A quick 'winter is coming' quip wouldn't have gone amiss. Yet, just when we think Rankin is missing obvious cultural references we note he's clearly seen *Iron Man*.

5) Although this has nothing to do with *Even Dogs in The Wild* Rankin on the publicity circuit did reveal at last who he thinks John Rebus resembles. He went for French actor Thierry Godard (Manchester event - November 2015). We'll wait while you google him... Now the first thing to say is we thing this is bang on and pretty close to our ideas. It must also be said that as it's from the horse's mouth it has to be taken as definitive. He made the caveat that the older Rebus is probably closer to actor Brian Cox.

Firsts and lasts:

It's the last of the '5 word' titles. Now we confess that we missed this one for the first edition and Rankin himself pointed it out at an event in Manchester in November 2015. The title links are entirely coincidental but now they've noticed Rankin quite likes them. One gets the impression his publisher hates them.

First mention of modern glories emojis, Costa Coffee, angry birds, Starbucks and vaping. It's, we presume the last time Rebus retires and it's the last mention of the Scottish referendum, although we still don't know how Rebus voted – we're guessing he didn't. It's the first time we get any sort of age of Malcolm Fox, which is given as three years to retirement (theoretically). Working on a thirty year service and Fox joined after school that makes him 45. We'll come back to that in Things that don't make Sense. It's the first time for quite a while that Rankin shares the narrative widely, with Cafferty, Malcolm Christie, an unnamed criminal and Joe Stark all getting narrative duties. Although Rankin often frames books by days this is the first time he does it using 'Day 1' etc.

Background:

Rankin's sabbatical between *Saints of the Shadow Bible* and this is well documented. He elaborated more on the problem in the publicity for this book, which was panic attacks, but while he was having his year off his antenna kept twitching and the abiding image in his mind was of someone aiming a gun at Cafferty. He thought, 'what can I do with that?' The other idea in his head was an anecdote he was a told in a bar in a little village in Scotland and it was something that happened in that particular village. A suspected drug dealer had died of natural causes, but the rumour went around that he had buried a big stash of cash and drugs in the woods. And so over the weekend the villagers would take up shovels and forks and would all march to the woods and start digging in random spots to see if they could uncover this treasure trove, which they never did. All Rankin had to do was transfer the idea to Edinburgh and add various crime syndicates and the police. He also found time to visit Police Scotland's Crime Campus and found that the culture had completely changed from his last visit. He joked he told them off for making his life difficult. With the year of enforced absence in his way he champing at the bit until January 2015 and the first draft was written in ten days, the usual page 65 crisis wasn't a problem this time and he refined the work at his usual retreat in Cromarty. He sent a series of tweets teasing at the title 'being a song with a catchy chorus': not Dancing Queen etc. By April was on the road sussing out venues and tweeting about how he was actually working, honest.

He felt as he wrote it that the book was about mortality and the very sombre mood throughout the book is a reflection of that. Rankin was keen to emphasise that the book wasn't necessarily going to be a John Rebus book but if Cafferty was in it wasn't a huge leap to include the cop most closely associated with him.

The opening scene is very reminiscent of the classic *Sopranos* episode 'Pine Barrens' directed by Steve Buschemi. The set-up is essentially identical and the way the rest of the episode plays out is implied by the hoods later on. Again, whether this is deliberate or a coincidence is difficult to know. The abuse story at the heart of this book is similar in style to the stories emerging at the time about prominent figures in the UK using and abusing vulnerable children in care homes. The Greville Janner case was very prominent at the time and only fizzled out when Janner died in late 2015 and the spectre of Jimmy Savile's decades long abuse will long hang in the psyche of people of these islands. Yet, we have to say it, crime writers were almost queuing up to add such institutionalised child abuse tales to their oeuvre. On television the *Endeavour* episode 'Neverland' was broadcast in April 2014 and featured a very similar set-up. And they keep on coming, the 2016 Inspector Banks novel by Peter Robinson 'When the Music's Over' covers similar ground even if it is much less subtle than Rankin's take (we should also note that Robinson delayed time in his books and Inspector Banks is, it seems perennially in his early 50s). It's almost expected, yet Rankin was covering this stuff 16 years earlier in the excellent *Dead Souls*. If you take all this in and add to the mix the title and there is another theme of father and son relationships. The Starks of course, Fox and his dad, other ones we won't mention here for plot exposition reasons, and of course the fairly obvious point that Rebus is acting as a sort of surrogate father to Fox, trying to turn him into a proper cop. Rankin, ever the analyst suspects that as his own sons were leaving home age he was feeding off that. There was no intention of this theme, he noticed it during the editing process. All this blokeiness and father and son stuff means that Siobhan is rather sidelined and we hope this isn't a trend.

We were going to have a small moan at the lack of Edinburghness in this book too, but, we've decided we were being overly fannish. Although it's true that Rankin doesn't use the city like a character anymore there is still plenty of Edinburgh, it just isn't in your face. There's the Golden Rule pub, St. Bernard's Crescent, Newington Rd even has a garage full of hearses which has an almost Penny Lane feel about it. Rankin even gets a nod to jazz musician Tommy Smith into the book as an ex-resident of Wester Hailes, something he's mentioned in interviews before when he's justified making up sink hole estates, not using real ones.

Musical references:

Only a few this time: with Steve Miller band, Van Morrison, Rory Gallagher and Tom Waits CDs all having been played on Rebus date night. Oh and Rebus misses a James Blunt reference.

Things That Don't make sSense:

The prologue could do with a date at the top. We know this is a stylistic decision but as it's written (apart from the cassette clue) it has no links to the past in which it's set. Adding a date allows the reader to understand there's a lot more to this tale than the first 100 pages make out. Given (as we'll note in the verdict) that the book is a slow burner this could have kept the momentum. While we're in the prologue we're struggling to believe that two hoods would own a tape of an obscure first album by The Associates, especially in 1987 when not everything was available like it is now. Not many people did own this tape (and before you moan, the Greatest Hits came out after the events here.)

OK, so Malcolm Fox is somewhere between 45 and 48 with thirty years' experience of policing, does this unsure and naive character portrayed here really fit to that level of experience? Also Fox claims he tried snaring Rebus 'many a time' when he was in the Complaints. As we've noted before this is not something that ever occurred in the books. Fox was never mentioned of course. While we're vaguely on the subject although Siobhan's age is not mentioned she is still considered by Rankin to be hot stuff for single DI's in her thirties, as we've said before, she's probably in her mid 40's. Finally the 'chaste' romance between Fox and Siobhan...Come on...and this friendship actually holds the book together, as Fox's woes and story arc have nothing to do with the main plot.

Rebus recommends Siobhan listens to *Sailor Girl* by the Steve Miller Band and says its track 7 on the CD. Well that rules out that Rebus has the album it was on originally, where it was the first track on side 2 (or track 5 on the CD). On the Best of... it's track 11...

Although we love the part where Rebus wakes up Fox with a cafetiere of coffee that doesn't sound right to us. We feel he'd go for the instant.

Cafferty a septuagenarian computer novice can get the link between the cases in an instant on Google yet the DC Esson and the combined power of Scottish Police can't. We accept there are very good narrative reasons for it happen this way and it give a Rebus an 'in' to a story that desperately needs him, also of course Cafferty knows what he's looking for...also the main protagonists' job is a little coincidental. While we're on the subject we're not quite sure exactly what the CID team are actually doing for most of the book.

Verdict:

Voodoo Lounge, Around the Sun, Face Dances, Dig out your Soul: all late period albums by great bands. Often described as 'return to form' by reviewers but are promptly forgotten once the publicity subsides - until the next 'return to form'. Look, Ian Rankin is never going to write a bad book but this one is never going to make anyone's top five. There's no development of the Rebus character, what's left to develop? And the supporting cast show how much they still need him. The deft idea in *Standing in Another Man's Grave* of contrasting the dinosaur cop with the bland, efficient vanilla modern police officers has turned round and bitten him once he needs those bland characters to carry his series. I mean, can any of you think of *anything* memorable about DCI James Page? 10 books ago even the supporting cast had lives, but not here. Neither Fox, nor Clarke have partners, hobbies, vices, hooks, anything and we are going to need something soon. Even the hints at Siobhan's drinking don't go anywhere and should be treated with suspicion because it is through the eyes of tee-total Fox.

We're still convinced that Rankin doesn't like the modern world of policing. If you look at the team put on the Minton investigation they do very little in the way of sleuthing, or if you prefer none of the modern techniques are seen to be useful. These days the network of CCTV cameras make it virtually impossible not to. It reinforces the nagging feeling we have that Rankin should bite the bullet and set a Rebus story in the past. There were times reading this when we worried that finally Rankin had settled into cosy mode and this was a tread water job. It's easy to see why we thought this; the first proper attempt by Rankin to broaden the canvas and make Siobhan, Fox and Rebus co-stars and bringing in Cafferty and Christie as characters driving storylines. Whether Rankin likes it or not Malcolm Fox cannot carry a story on his own and in truth (nor can Clarke). So Rebus gets the majority of the sleuthing and very good he is at it too. There are still neat ideas here: like the car parks of previous books, the hook idea here is very plausible, we're just not going to mention it…

Which is the problem: the emotional power and weight of this very good book comes from the old duo Cafferty and Rebus. The book crackles when they are centre stage and lulls when they're not. The sleuthing is great here but the killer is found by another whopping coincidence and there's an argument that the unique selling point here is so common recently that this is old hat, yet Rankin brings a sadness to the narrative it we've rarely seen before.

What order should you read the Rebus books?

On twitter Rankin suggests either knots and crosses or black and blue. My list is:

Set in Darkness
Black and Blue
Fleshmarket Close
Let it Bleed
Hide and Seek
Tooth and Nail
Dead Souls
The Falls
Resurrection Men
A Question of Blood
Knots and Crosses
Strip Jack
The Black Book
Hanging Garden
Mortal Causes
The Naming of the Dead
Exit Music
Standing in Another Man's Grave
Saints of the Shadow Bible
Even Dogs in the Wild

Afterword by Ray Dexter

The first time I visited the Oxford bar was a heart in the mouth moment. I had never been before but I was visiting Nadine who was living in Edinburgh and decided to pay the place a visit. I paced outside for a few minutes remembering Rankin's anecdote that barman doesn't serve the English, and my accent is particularly English (for my sins). Finally I summoned up the courage walked into the tiny front bar area and ordered a pint of heavy with few problems. Given the size of the front area and all the stools were occupied by TV watching regulars I went into the backroom. It was empty save for me. I drank my beer and looked around taking pictures on my phone and just trying to imagine where Rebus (or Rankin) chose to sit. I went for the table furthest away from the door facing the entrance – very Rebusy. As I supped I marvelled at how right it felt in here, here brilliantly Rankin conveyed the place without going into too much detail, getting the patrons right rather than ornate descriptions. It was one of my favourite afternoons.

This is what Ian Rankin is great at, describing locations with such style that physical descriptions of characters are rarely needed. That said, a visit to the Ox is a must for any Rankin fan.

We wrote this book because we love Ian Rankin's work and we love John Rebus, but we also wanted a book that was accessible and celebrated the work rather than focused too much on the academic allusions. We hope you like it.

Although this book is unofficial and unauthorized, we would like to thank Ian Rankin for being so forthcoming in interviews over the years. He never seems to tire of talking about Rebus and the writing process and even better for us he rarely contradicts himself. Without such openness, a book like this would have been far harder to write.

We would also like to thank St Edmund's College, Ware for its help in the preparation of this book.

Finally, as promised the link to access the picture of the flat in Arden Street.

http://www.dailyrecord.co.uk/news/scottish-news/home-address-ian-rankins-famous-1898109

Printed in Great Britain
by Amazon

13236248R00122